If you have a home computer with internet access you may:
-request an item be placed on hold
-renew an item that is overdue
-view titles and due dates checked out on your card
-view your own outstanding fines

To view your patron record from your home computer:
Click on the NSPL homepage:
http://nspl.suffolk.lib.ny.us

North Shore Public Library

the curse of FOUR

the CURSE of FOUR

A Black London Novella

CAITLIN KITTREDGE

Subterranean Press 2011

First Edition

ISBN
978-1-59606-398-3

Subterranean Press
PO Box 190106
Burton, MI 48519

www.subterraneanpress.com

*"Indubitably, Magic is one of the subtlest and
most difficult of the sciences and arts.
There is more opportunity for errors of comprehension, judgment
and practice than in any other branch of physics."*
—Aleister Crowley

"I'm going to tell you the secret of magic: any cunt can do it."
—Alan Moore

one

THERE are plenty of ghosts in London, if you know where to look. From the Romans on, London has belonged to the dead, been built upon them. The living walk on the ashes of the old city, burned down and built up by conquest, fire, war and time. The Blitz alone took more than forty-three thousand souls, and centuries of plague, fighting and poverty before stacked the dead thick and fast upon the ground.

Every nook and cranny of the city teems with the dead. You feel them, a vague discomfort, a patch of cold, a feeling you can't pin down except to know that it isn't yours. You can smell the dead, taste them, ashes and dust on your tongue in the dark corners and underground places of London. You can see them, tattered clothing and empty eyes, filmstrips of misery preserved and looped forever on the screen of the magic, the energy, the blood and bone of their city.

You can see the dead. If you know where to look.

Jack Winter had lived the balance of his life trying not to look. Like whipping your head away just at the most frightening

---

part of a horror film, he tried not to see the dead. But the dead saw him. They always did, sooner or later. A man with his talent was like a bright beacon of light in the darkest place on earth, a lamprey for spirits.

Various things blunted the sight, but blunting did fuck-all when sight was mingled with a touch of magic in the blood— not much, just enough to make things interesting and turn him into BBC One for every psychic impression in greater London. Heroin had blinded it, for a good long while, but you couldn't stay willfully blind to the world around you forever. Not unless you wanted to wake up one morning and find yourself with your eyes put out.

Jack hunched inside his coat, the only passenger on his section of pavement in the Mile End Road. Whitechapel, never much of a tourist destination even in the blush of spring, closed up tight at night. The pubs were still busy, but the punters were shut in with the warmth except for a few tenacious smokers rattling inside their anoraks and swearing at the Chelsea-Liverpool game running silent on the telly inside.

He passed closed-up stalls where his neighbors sold vegetables, knockoff handbags, prepaid mobile phones and everything else a burgeoning immigrant neighborhood could want during the day, and crossed against the light to the block that contained his flat.

Ginger Annie stood on the corner, and she turned to him with a slow, warm smile that went miles toward keeping out the cold. "Hello, luv. You look near frozen."

"Annie." Jack tipped his head to her, keeping it professional. That was really the only way it could go between reluctant psychic and ghost.

"I could keep you warm." Annie stretched out a hand to him. Parts of her faded from color to silver and back, a faulty celluloid reel. Ash and soot decorated the pale gray of her skin, a deep wound marring the copper river of hair that now was done up in elaborate victory rolls, now was matted with blood and tangled in bits of her battered skull. "So warm," Annie promised. "The best you've ever felt."

"You know," Jack told her, stopping to light a cigarette. A touch of his finger and the cherry glowed to life, the first hit stinging his lungs with heat, "a nice girl like you really shouldn't be out so late, Annie."

She laughed. It was like fingers on his bare skin. "Jack. You know I'm not that nice."

Ginger Annie had been killed in 1942, when a pimp by the name of Lyle McReady, by all accounts an arse-faced tosser if there ever was one, stove her skull in with the heel of his boot. Even in the blue-collar crush of the East End, violent bloody murder wouldn't normally go overlooked, but fortunately for McReady a German V2 rocket had demolished the building where he'd stashed Annie's body. She still stood on her corner, the only white face now amid the usual ebb and flow of Jack's Bangladeshi and Pakistani neighbors, waiting patiently for a smile, a kind word, a customer she could touch and whisper to and steal a little warmth from.

Annie never killed the living she came into contact with, which was more than Jack could say for a lot of nasty-cunt creatures he'd come across in his life, so they had come to a sort of agreement, which was mostly that Jack left her alone and she left him alone, except for nights like tonight. She'd told him once it had been very cold when she died. "I could feel my own blood getting cold on my face. Do you have any idea what that feels like?"

In the winter, she was always extra chatty.

Jack exhaled. "I'll be going, then. You take care, Annie."

Her fingers trailed across his leather as he walked on, a set of pinpricks on his body and on the part of his mind where his talent lived, that strange ephemeral tether to the Black, the place where magic and all of the things that came with it lived, the London that was not London and at the same time more London than the city of the living could ever be. The Black was what any normal person forgot, resigned to nightmares and took pills to avoid. To Jack, it was the closest thing he'd ever had to a home.

Still, a psychic with amplified receivers had a piss-poor time in an active area, which was why he stayed in Whitechapel even as his whiter, posher friends expressed horror at the idea. A potter's field for the Romans, who burned their dead to the east of the City, a slum soaked in the blood and misery of eighty thousand souls during the reign of Victoria, and finally a borderland between the stratospheric wealth of those who lived beyond the wall in the original square mile and the slow, inexorable growth and metastization of the suburbs beyond, Whitechapel was a place with a dark heart and a darker shadow, one that muted the roar of the Black and usually enabled Jack to at least sleep, if not soundly.

A neighborhood faded and worn down but still ready to kick you in the teeth, he'd rather liked Whitechapel when he'd landed in London at fourteen, and he still liked it enough to keep his decaying prewar flat, one of the few not flattened by Hitler's bombs, in at least a semblance of livability.

Having a flatmate who was both female and a former detective inspector for the Met helped with the last bit, as well. But Pete was in Cornwall, looking at cows or eating pasties or getting mauled by inbred Cornish folk with incomprehensible accents—whatever it was that regular people did to unwind from a hectic city life.

Jack supposed he had better at least do the washing up before she came back, if only to conceal the fact he'd been living on takeaway and cigarettes. Not that Pete was much better—she'd been a workaholic copper for most of her adult life without time for domestic faffing about, and could sniff out a superior curry in any neighborhood in London with alarming accuracy.

But she'd fuss over him, and Jack didn't want her to think he was completely incapable of being civilized, even though every girlfriend he'd ever had accused him of it at some point, and even his mate Lawrence characterized his general lifestyle as "bloody disgusting and askin' for a heart attack sooner rather than later."

The lift in his building was permanently out of order, or working just well enough to cause Jack to fear for his life if he got inside the gated, gear-driven contraption, so he took the stairs, huffing up four flights with his cigarette clamped between his lips.

Really, Pete was a remarkably easy person to live with. She didn't nag and she didn't hover, and she knew the value of silence. He was fucking lucky to have her. In more ways than one. But not in a sense that involved literal fucking, because Pete wasn't that kind of a girl. Disappointing as that was on nights when Jack was restless and wishing he were twenty-five and in a band again. It had been so dead easy then he'd laughed at himself.

Even Pete hadn't been immune to his charms. Not then.

Jack shouldered open the stairwell door, rippled glass painted with an Art Deco rendering of *Fourth Floor*. And stopped dead, body and thought.

A shadow waited, at his door. It was a long shadow, heavy and solid. It was attached to a figure in a dark coat, head tucked down, just a blob of blackness in the dingy light of Jack's hallway.

His head wasn't pounding with an incipient attack of the sight, so it likely wasn't a dead thing. Nor were his mage senses flaring as they mingled with the magic of something bigger and badder than him, so a demon was out.

That was a relief. Demon vs. mage never ended well for the mage. Usually it just plain ended. Often with your head separated from your body and you with a stupid look on your face.

Jack didn't catch any ambient power, the mage's version of a pissing contest—*Whip it out, son, and let's measure.* He did a quick mental inventory of who was slagged off at him this week. Mad Tim was still upset about Jack borrowing one of his grimoires and bringing it back with tea stains. Kate Hamal thought he was a sexist pig because he'd gotten drunk at Hallow's Eve and grabbed her arse, but Kate Hamal was a self-righteous, politically correct bint who spelled *magic* with a K. The various other gangsters, hard men and black magicians that Jack had crossed paths with since he'd emerged from his smack haze were, at the moment, none of his concern.

So the man at the door was an unknown quantity. Human, but unknown. Jack fucking hated working with unknown variables. He felt in the pocket of his leather for his flick-knife. The jacket and the blade were the two holdovers from his days as a filthy punk, along with his steel-toed engineer boots. The jacket was a statement, the boots a practicality. Most things of flesh, both in London and the Black, were not immune to having the shit kicked out of them. And if you looked like a scary mad bastard while doing it, so much the better.

Jack held the blade down so it opened against his leg, muting the *click*. The blade's handle was smooth black enamel, and it warmed under his palm.

He took a step from the stairwell, putting his feet on the threadbare runner. The floor was creaky, but Jack wasn't planning to take his sweet time.

He could use magic, of course. But magic took time, and energy. Spells could go awry. Besides, a gangly blond twat waving his arms about and chanting just wasn't intimidating, no matter how you looked at it.

Jack moved, and the man's shape lifted away from the wall. Jack caught the shine of wide eyes before he hooked one arm around the man's neck, pulling them back to front and using the leverage of his momentum to press his forearm against the fatter man's windpipe.

He placed the knife against the man's face, scraping it against his orbital bone so his uninvited guest could see the blade.

"Right," Jack breathed in his ear. "You've got three seconds to tell me why you're skulking 'round my door, mate, before I give you a second mouth so you can sing duet."

"For fuck's sake, Winter," Ollie Heath grunted. "I just want to talk to you."

Jack loosened his grip a fraction, but he didn't move the knife. "DI Heath. What the fuck are you doing here?"

"I'll tell you if you get that bloody knife out of my eye, you paranoid cunt," Ollie gasped.

"Not enough," Jack said. Heath was Pete's old partner from her Met days, but there were limits. "I don't like cops at my fucking threshold, Oliver." That was true enough—no one who grew up on the poor side of Manchester in the 1980s liked police, of any stripe. And they didn't come much more sanctimonious in Jack's mind than Ollie Heath.

"Oh, fuck off," Ollie sighed, and Jack was visited with a stabbing pain in his gut as Ollie elbowed him and broke free. He did some kind of flash police throw that put Jack on the ground, hard, and when Jack looked up again he was facing the business end of a 9mm pistol. Jack grinned.

"You checked out your firearm to come see little old me? I'm flattered, Ollie."

"Yeah, well." Ollie holstered the thing awkwardly in his armpit and straightened his rumpled trench coat in a khaki hump over his belly. "Haven't met many bastards I'd like to shoot more than you, Winter."

He offered Jack a hand up. Jack shot him the bird and got to his feet, making his flick-knife disappear from his palm and secreting it back into a pocket. Heath blinked at the trick, half magic and half clever fingers. "You're pretty good with that sleight of hand bullshit, I'll give you that."

Jack unlocked the door of the flat and briefly toyed with the idea of inviting Heath in and then letting the protection hex that Jack kept over the flat eat him. "What do you want, Ollie?"

Heath followed Jack inside as if the place belonged to him. "To talk. Like I said while you was attacking me like some kind of nutty little ASBO. You've got problems, Winter."

"Not news to me." Jack slung his leather onto the coat rack and brought his pack of Parliaments along to the sitting room. "Right now, me biggest one is a fat fucking policeman standing in my flat." He slumped onto the sofa and put his boots up, making sure he gave Ollie plenty of time to take the place in. The occult books and handwritten grimoires piled in every corner, the things preserved in jars, the ceremonial bone dagger that Jack had taken off a Stygian Brother in a card game nearing twenty years ago. Let the busybodied fuck know he wasn't in his element, and get him squirming. "Talk, Heath," he said in his most grating Northern brogue. "Ain't got all fuckin' night, do I?"

Ollie stood in the center of the carpet, hands hanging loose at his sides, as if he were being called out before the headmaster of the private school he'd undoubtedly attended.

"I caught a homicide a few days ago," he said at last.

"Good lad," Jack replied. "My revenue at work."

Ollie's jaw twitched. "Will you let me finish? You never fucking listen. That's what Pete says."

That one got Jack to think for a second. "Pete talks to you? About me?"

"In case you hadn't noticed, Winter," Ollie said, "you didn't leave her with a lot of friends when you dragged her into your sordid little lifestyle."

Ollie folded his arms, and there was something, a new steel in his spine, that Jack had never witnessed. He'd always figured

Heath for a career middleman, somebody who was content to take orders from a slightly less gray middleman and plod his way to the grave on a steady diet of bad coffee, worse food and the dregs of humanity killing one another off. Pete had definitely been the shining star of their partnership. Her father, DI Connor Caldecott, was a legend in his time, and even though Jack had always thought the Irish bastard was a pompous arse, he had to admit the man was fucking good at his job. He'd passed his skills to Pete, and before she'd left to pursue the esoteric side of her talents, she'd been a fucking good DI as well. Heath was just a middle-aged bloke in a bad suit who was never quite quick enough, smart enough or fit enough to close the big case, the career-makers that got you plum assignments and promotions.

"I don't put stock in this sort of thing." Ollie encompassed the odds and ends of Jack's trade with one hand. "But I've come up against something that I can't fully explain, any way I poke it or prod it or stick it under a microscope." He lowered his head, breathed in and out, and then met Jack's eyes. "I'd...*appreciate* it if you'd take a look at the crime scene and my files and tell me what you think."

Jack took a moment to *appreciate* how much it was clearly wearing on Heath to ask him for help. "What is it, then?" he said aloud. "Weekend Satanists? Stage magician get topped by one of his tricks? I'm not a walking Wikipedia of the fucking strange to make your job easier, Heath. I'm busy."

He wasn't, at the moment—exorcisms, the thing that usually put tea on the table, had run dry and none of his mates who worked in the Black had thrown any work his way in months. It was cold. Things that might need a mage's skills were hibernating, and they were living on Pete's savings. But that wasn't any of Heath's bloody business.

Ollie kept staring him down. It was rather unnerving, to see those hard eyes staring out of the blandly pleasant Yorkshire-pudding face. "I think a girl was killed by a ghost."

That made Jack sit up. Ghosts could bother the living, certainly. Poltergeists could fling things at your head and revenants could claw you to ribbons, but the dead usually didn't have the wherewithal to actually, physically murder.

"You think?" Jack said. "You mean you're willing to consider maybe I'm not just some lying tosser trying to get into your partner's knickers?" He smirked. "Real progress, Heath. Next you'll be admitting you believe in Santa Claus."

He was being a cunt, but men like Heath had always rubbed him the wrong way. The Good Men, Jack called them. Men who were so convinced of their own virtue they couldn't help seeing all other men as wickedly substandard.

Not that Jack argued with the designation. He wasn't angelic. He wasn't even basically decent.

He also wasn't prepared for Heath to close the distance between them, leaning into Jack's face, breathing out the smell of pie and lager. "Listen," Ollie said. "I don't like you. I don't like you and I don't fucking trust you. You're a lowlife piece of shit and Pete could do worlds better. But a girl is dead, and it's on me to find the doer and give her family that peace. So are you going to help me, or are you really the sociopathic block of ice I think you are, deep down?"

Jack didn't break eye contact, didn't give Heath that satisfaction of flinching. "You really want my help, Ollie?" he said.

"Then you'll accept my help. You won't piss all over my explanation for whatever happened to the dead girl. You won't just use me to salve your conscience so you can close the file, all right?"

Heath stepped back, smoothing his hands over his coat, which did precisely nothing for the wrinkles and gravy stain down the front. "Yes, all right. That's all I wanted, Winter. Pete's right. You're fucking difficult."

"Born that way," Jack said. "Not going to change."

"I'll pick you up tomorrow," Heath said, going to the door. "Nine or so. We'll drive over to the scene."

"Nine?" Jack said. "Christ, Heath, are you trying to kill me?"

"Now there's a lovely thought," Heath said. "Nine a.m., Winter. Don't be a cunt about it."

two

HEATH'S car, unlike Pete's red vintage Mini Cooper, was about as unimaginative as you could get, even for a cop. Ollie drove the black Vauxhall like an old woman, too, staying under the speed limit and slowing for changing lights.

Jack swigged at his takeaway coffee and winced. "Bloody hell, Heath. While we're still young."

"Your job is to evaluate the crime scene," Ollie gritted. "My job is the drivin'."

"You do a good job of it, you know," Jack said. "Hiding the accent. Sounding like you came from the same place all of those other middle-class fucks did. You don't need to let it make you so tense."

Ollie stared ahead resolutely as the lorry in front of them lurched into motion. "Don't know what you're on about."

"Pete told me you're from Yorkshire," Jack said. "But it's not just the dirty North, is it? You're a big strapping lad. You grow up on farmer food, Ollie? You drive a tractor and sling sheep around with mud on your boots?"

Ollie's nostrils flared. "Stop that mind-reader shite right now, Winter. You don't know me."

"I can't read your mind," Jack said. "Talent doesn't work that way. I can just read you."

"Bullshit you can," Ollie muttered. "There's no mud on me."

"Look," Jack said. "I grew up on the worst council estate in Manchester. My mother was one step above a whore because she only did it for pills, not for cash. I wore the shabbiest clothes, and Mum's impressive string of sociopathic meal tickets beat seven kinds of hell out of me every day until I left. I wished for a long bloody time I could just wash it all off, but you can't wash that kind of psychic imprint off, ever. It's your skin. Trust me, Heath. Life gets a fuck of a lot easier if you simply make peace with it."

Ollie jerked the car to the curb, snapping Jack against his seat belt. "We're here." He egressed the car with impressive speed for a fat man, and strode over to a block of flats that had been cordoned off with police tape.

Jack didn't push it. It wasn't his business if Heath wanted to pretend he was the same kind of wanker as all the other wankers in the Met.

He threw the rest of the vile coffee into the gutter and followed Heath, ducking the tape and skipping the front step. Heath was standing in the entry hall, hands in his pockets, just looking.

"So let's see the last breathing spot of the dearly departed," Jack said. Nothing in the building was pinging his mental alarms, but there was a shiver here, the slightest rend in the fabric of the Black. Something had come and gone, and left the layers of power a house collected vibrating, like a tube train had just passed below his feet.

the curse of FOUR

"I want to warn you," Ollie said as they started up the staircase. "This isn't pretty. Even with the body gone, it's a crime scene, and it's one that people down at the MIT are still talking about. Bloody. Bad and bloody."

"I have seen dead things before, Heath," Jack said. "'M not going to vomit all over your evidence."

"I don't care if you spew your bloody liver out your nose," Heath said. "Just do it elsewhere."

He climbed the stairs, which groaned under his tread. Jack followed, that leak of psychic malignancy growing stronger, a current rather than a trickle, as he climbed up into the bones of the old building.

They were in Spitalfields, a warren of alleys and side streets that until a hundred years ago had been the hunting ground of the sort of predators who walked on two legs and smiled as they cut your throat. Now the falling-down real estate was worth a fortune and the world at large recognized the place from the insipid CGI vistas of Harry Potter. But there were still pockets of the old city, here and everywhere in London. You could paint her over and tart her up and parade her out good as new, a post-Thatcher, post-millennium whore, but sooner or later, she'd be up to her old tricks. You could cover up the scars, but you could never erase them. A thousand years of fire and poverty and madness don't wash off. They wound in the threads of the city, bright lines of power against the background static of the Black. And they vibrated here, in this dank bleach-scented hallway of this dank, depressing little flat block. Vibrated with something awful, something that had cut the lines like a razor.

Ollie ducked underneath more yellow tape and opened the door of the first flat on the right. He moved like a cop, keeping his back against the door frame, eyes sweeping the interior until he was satisfied they were alone. The movements weren't very natural on his tubby frame, and Jack suppressed a smile. Wouldn't be very proper at a crime scene.

Then he stepped into the flat, and his urge to smile vanished all together.

The blood was the first, most immediate thing that caught Jack's attention. There was a pool of it on the threadbare Persian rug in the single large room—it was the sort of rug an arty girl might go out and find herself at a jumble sale, and count herself lucky she did. The stain was the size of a small country, and Jack had seen blood before, blood in all amounts and spilled for all reasons, but there was something about the girl-sized stain and the spatter that drilled into his mind like needles, the psychic echo of her last moments ricocheting inside his skull.

Blood was on the walls, on the shabby Asda furniture. A fine long spray, the dying tremor of an artery, or a fat vein, spread across the wallpaper and the sofa, staining the flowers and the oatmeal fabric—tasteful, bland, like everything else in the room—with a final stroke.

"It happened right here," Ollie said. "Her throat was cut. No sign of forced entry, doors and windows locked from the inside. He didn't come in and he didn't leave, 'least not according to the forensics report. No prints except hers. Not a fucking thing."

Jack dug his fingers into his right eyebrow, massaged the spot underneath as it started to throb. There wasn't just blood in this place. There was leakage, a toxic spill that permeated every level of his consciousness. Something had been here—wasn't any longer, thank fuck—and had left a screaming tear behind it. Something dead, and angry, and full of the hunger of the angry dead. It grabbed at Jack's sight, clawed it, left bloody red marks all through his brain.

There was warm and wet on his upper lip and Ollie grimaced, then handed him a tissue. "You all right, Winter?"

Jack scrubbed at the blood dribbling from his nose. A spirit hadn't hit him like that in a long time. "Your girl didn't get topped by accident," he said. "Whatever's in here, it takes calling. Calling from somebody who knows what they're doing." He shoved the tissue into his pocket. "This girl have any enemies?"

Ollie took out his PDA and flipped through his notes screen by screen. "Name was Fiona Hannigan," he said. "Thirty-one years old. Irish citizen, no relatives, in the UK on a work visa—expired, by the by. Worked around the corner in a record shop..."

Heath ran on, but Jack didn't hear him and eventually Heath stopped reading off his screen. "Winter, what's wrong with you? You dodgy? Pete said you were off the dope."

Jack shook his head. He was damp inside his leather, a cold damp that came from brushing too close against the sort of spirit that lingered here. "I have to get out of here," he muttered, his innards rebelling like he'd just spent the night in his favorite absinthe bar in Paris.

He made it as far as the planter urn in the hallway before he threw up.

Heath followed him, and had the manners not to comment until Jack managed to draw in a breath and swipe the back of his hand across his mouth. "I did warn you, Winter. If you're not used to looking at these things they can sneak up on you."

"It's not that," Jack managed. The spirit was one thing—Jack could deal with bad spirits, the hungry dead, even if it felt like taking a pipe to the forehead. It wasn't any ghost that had caused the rolling in his guts.

"Then what?" Ollie said. "Because if you've got the bloody bird flu, stay the fuck away from me."

"No…" Jack pulled up the tail of his Ruts shirt and swiped it across his face. "Fiona Hannigan. I knew her."

three

THE London city mortuary was a sterile place. Jack had always imagined it was as twisty, warren-like and poorly lit as the rest of the secret places in the city, but the mortuary was if anything overly bright, staffed by the sort of chipper, efficient government types that set his teeth on edge and decorated in the same flat, muted tones one finds at the dole office, designed to keep the unruly masses docile. Polite signs directed him to *Receiving, Pathology* and *Restrooms.*

Ollie was beyond the swinging doors, where they kept the corpses.

It wasn't Jack's first mortuary—that had been Amsterdam, at nineteen, when his mate Billy Ames had OD'd and Jack was the only one straight enough to claim the body. Billy Ames hadn't been a mage, just a stupid fucking musician, but you never forget your first.

Fiona Hannigan. Jesus. How many years had it been?

The chair Ollie had pointed him to was hard, making the pyramid studs on his belt dig into his kidneys and leaving his legs with nowhere to go but into the hallway, where a pathologist in a smart set of pink scrubs glared at him as she sidestepped.

"Wait here, Winter," Heath said with the smugness that men like him only found on their home turf. "I'll see about you viewing the body."

Jack had stayed quiet on the ride over. Other than asking to see Fiona, he hadn't said a word.

Whatever had killed Fiona Hannigan, it wasn't human. And it was looking like she'd brought it on herself. Jack had convinced Heath he could get a better read if he could put eyes on the corpse, which was sometimes true. The dead left their flesh behind like so much discarded rubbish, but magic clings to flesh, like cigarette smoke to skin after a long night in a shite bar.

The fluorescent lights were giving Jack a worse headache than he'd already brought on himself smacking into the residue of the power in Fiona's flat, and Jack buried his head in his hands, nearly missing the footsteps that stopped in front of him.

"Don't you look a sight."

He snapped his head up. "Pete."

She stood before him, her overcoat draped over one arm and her bag slung over her shoulder. Pete's skin was extraordinarily pale, her Black Irish father and the mother she'd never clapped eyes on combining to churn out a pair of fairy-princess sisters, one budding and velvety as a rose and one slender and immovable as an oak.

A frown line dug into the space between Pete's eyes. "Who the fuck else would come find you in a mortuary with a bunch of coppers, Jack? Not any of your fucking friends, that's for sure."

Jack sighed, suddenly needing a smoke and about a gallon of whiskey. "How'd you know I was nicked?"

"Ollie called me, didn't he," Pete replied. "We do still talk, you know." She shrugged her bag, still heavy with her overnight kit, to the floor. "He said you'd been to a crime scene and you were a bit rattled. After I got through ripping him a new arsehole for taking you anywhere near his investigation in the first place, I had to come see what has Jack fucking Winter rattled. It's a new experience."

"You came all the way from Cornwall just now?" Jack said. "Fuck me, does the Mini have a built-in TARDIS I don't know about?"

Pete shrugged, softening her posture a tad. "Fuck it. I was on my way home anyway. Never did stomach the country."

Jack rubbed a hand over his face. He'd stopped trembling and sweating like a wino with end-stage DTs, at least. "I need to see the body. Heath said he had to ask permission from mummy or some bollocks. Been sitting here for fucking hours. Me arse is numb."

"Thank you for that," Pete said, but she was smiling. This was the Pete he was used to. She might take the piss from him on a regular basis, and she'd never taken any of his shit, even when she was a teenager and he was the unauthorized, secret Older Man, but Pete was constant. She had, in the words of his American friend Trish Grimes, his back.

Thinking of Trish just made him think of Fiona again, and he swallowed the lump of bile that welled at the memory. "Care to sit with me, luv?"

"Fuck that," Pete said, grabbing his hand. "Come with me." She was down the hall and through the swinging doors before

Jack could protest, and he let himself be dragged. It was usually easier to go along with Pete. She was half his size and three times as stubborn.

The smell hit Jack in the face when the air rushed back at them from the doors—disinfectant and bleach and the sweet odor of formaldehyde. Death-smell. Forget decomposition or rot, this was the scent of the dead. Jack's nose tingled and he swiped at it like a City banker after his lunchtime coke rasher.

An attendant sitting behind a desk barring regular people from the corpses looked up with the censorious frown of a prison warden, but he blinked when he saw Pete. "Fuck me, Caldecott. What are you doing here?"

"Your wife might have something to say about that," Pete returned, and Jack could tell by their smiles there was history. "How are you keeping yourself, Sunil?"

"You know," the attendant shrugged. "One foot in front of the other. You? Heard you quit this mad place."

"Traded it for another," Pete said with a chin-jerk at Jack. "Just as mad."

Sunil looked Jack over, and Jack felt a reflexive snarl at the clear judging he was receiving. "Ah," was all Sunil said.

"So the Hannigan bird," Pete segued. "You know the one, Irish girl, all cut up, came in about a week ago?"

"Yeah?" Sunil said cautiously. "What about her?"

"How about giving us a look?" Pete said. "For old time's sake."

Sunil's mouth crimped. "You know I can't do that, Pete. Not even for my favorite ex DI."

Jack snorted at that. The bloke obviously had a crush, and he was also obviously oblivious to the smart tune Pete was playing at that crush's expense. Pete jammed her elbow into his ribs, and Jack managed to go back to the blank and vaguely hostile face he'd cultivated when he was still young enough to receive regular attention from the coppers.

"Come on, Sunil," Pete wheedled. "It'd be doing me a fucking solid. Think of it as karma or something if it helps."

"Fuck you," Sunil said with a grin, shooting Pete the bird. "She's in drawer thirteen. Be gone before my supervisor gets back from lunch."

Pete gave Sunil a sunny, genuine smile and reached across the desk to pat him on the hand. Jack thought he gave a heroic effort in not rolling his eyes. Sunil was going to have wank fodder for weeks after that exchange.

Jack followed Pete into the room where a row of floor-to-ceiling freezers stared back at him like some nightmarish, alien chessboard. Computer-generated cards were tucked into a fair few of the drawers, names and surnames and date of death, others simply reading JOHN DOE. Some went back five years or more. Jack whistled. "They let them hang about this long?"

"Cold cases," Pete said. "No pun intended. You can keep a body for about ten years before it starts to degrade beyond usability. Particularly nasty ones, the medical examiner's crew usually holds them on ice."

Jack wondered, if he didn't find out what the fuck had happened to her, if Fiona Hannigan would rate such treatment.

"Any of yours?" he said, gesturing at the drawers. Pete shook her head.

"Fuck no. I close my cases. All the murders, anyway." She yanked open the drawer marked 13 in block numbers.

Jack hadn't expected a jolt at this part, but seeing the small form covered in sheeting caused his empty stomach to leap again. He needed to get a grip. He'd seen plenty of dead people, enough so that this part shouldn't be shocking any longer.

Pete rolled the sheet back from her face, and sighed. "She was pretty."

Was being the operative word. Fiona Hannigan was blue around the edges, all of the sheen and verve gone out of her carrot-orange hair and milky skin. There was no spirit there to trouble Jack. Fiona Hannigan was well and truly gone.

"How'd you know her?" Pete said. She was standing away, giving Jack his space. He wished she wouldn't leave him alone with Fiona.

He could lie, but Pete would spot it. She was a champion liar herself.

"I knew her the same way I knew any girl when I was twenty-two and fucking stupid," he answered.

Pete ripped the sheet off the rest of the way, far less gently. "Of course." Then, when she took in Fiona's bare body, "Jesus."

"That git's got fuck-all to do with this," Jack said. Fiona's body had been washed by the medical examiner, but it merely threw the stab wounds on her abdomen into sharp relief, black slits that gaped up at him from Fiona's ghostly pale skin. They were precise cuts, all in a row, no hesitation and no missing.

Pete paged through the report she'd hunted up from the file cabinet in the corner. "Says she cracked her head against the occasional table. Got a nasty concussion. Probably how he incapacitated her."

Jack was still looking at the cuts. Gut wounds were painful and slow. He'd wanted Fiona to hurt, wanted her to bleed, and wanted her to be alive while he did it, so she could watch. Then when he got tired of it, he'd finished it with the deep, black grin under her jaw where the knife had bisected her throat.

"Looks like she died hard," Pete said. "You need anything else, or can we get out of here? The dead people room always gave me the spooks."

Jack reached out, slowly, touching with just the pads of his fingers first to make sure he wasn't going to fry himself with psychic feedback, and put his hand over Fiona's. "Give us a minute, yeah?"

"Sure," Pete said, and backed out of the room.

Jack stayed perfectly still, not even breathing, letting the hum of the refrigeration unit and the buzz of the tube lighting overhead fill him up. Letting the cold of Fiona's skin spread to his. Letting the memories come.

He'd met Fiona Hannigan after a Poor Dead Bastards show in Aberdeen. She'd been years younger and pounds lighter, that acerbic, cigarette-smoking skinny that aspiring models like her all held in common. She was too short, though, and too lively— the red hair and the snapping eyes and the foul mouth all off-putting to paying work.

Jack had found her charming. So charming that after he escorted her back to the shitty hotel room meant for two, the room that he, Rich, Gavin and Dix were crashing in together, had kicked them out for the evening with their own company, had gotten her undressed and gotten on with business...so charming that he let her stay the night and woke up to find her smoking, naked, in the window in the light of dawn.

You're one in a million, Jack Winter, she'd exhaled with the blue halo of cheap fags. *Aren't you?*

Rich had a fiancée and Dix had three serious girlfriends that he kept spinning like so many plates, so it wasn't so very odd when Fiona began popping up at every show, appearing at whatever dark hole Jack was spending the night in, and doing things to him that every man thinks are just the pipe dreams of porno directors until they actually happen.

It wasn't so very odd when Fiona asked Jack if he'd like to meet her friends. They were having a party in Birmingham the same night the Bastards were playing.

It wasn't so very odd when she gave him a hit of something plant-based and strong enough to paint the face of God on the walls. Mescaline, Jack discovered that evening, was not his hallucinogen of choice.

It wasn't so very odd until Jack got to the warehouse where Fiona's friends were holding their party, all candles in clumps on every surface, pretty pierced boys hanging from chains via the rings in their backs, free-flowing, blood-dark alcohol that tasted like berries and bitter iron, and saw through his pleasant, muzzy haze that Fiona's friends were into some fairly heavy-duty sex magic.

The leader was a bloke who introduced himself as Chester, long greasy hair dyed black as a roomful of cats, bare chest with some bullshit alchemical symbols tattooed on, black leather pants, too much metal in his lips and nipples for Jack to think getting close to him could be anything but uncomfortable for his followers.

But Chester loved Jack. All of Fiona's friends loved Jack. All of them, with the exception of Chester, were entirely normal or had a bare spark of ability, the kind of thing their granny would call "sixth sense" that let them know when it was going to rain or who was on the other end of the phone.

They loved Jack. They wanted to touch him, to taste him, to hook him up to their rituals like a fucking transformer, a real live mage they could fuck into oblivion to do whatever-it-was that Chester had in mind. Jack was too fucked up to really hear him. He had a notion it had to do with demons, transformative ritual, as it almost always did when you ran into black magic cocksuckers.

Not that Jack was so very good and innocent. There were still a few brothers of the *Fiach Dubh,* the crow brothers who were his first refuge after he started seeing ghosts, who would have gladly stove in his face back in those days.

But he sure as hell wasn't doping up innocent people and raping them until he got a contact high to work his rituals, that was for fucking sure. He wasn't opening up his willing partners to possession, ghost sickness or worse.

Jack wondered, as he looked down at Fiona's still face, why after that first night he hadn't simply run the fuck away.

Her, of course. Her too-wide mouth and her deep, deep eyes and that little-girl way she had of sitting in her short skirts so her knees knocked together. Tailor-made to turn men far more resolute than him into slobbering white knights.

Jack had sobered up and left Fiona resting on his futon, Chester's fingerprints still turning to bruises all over her, and he'd gone back to the man's flat. Woke him up, put him on the floor and threatened to take a straight razor to his balls if he didn't let Fiona go.

Chester had actually laughed at him, but he'd said fine, all yours, good hunting mate.

And Fiona hadn't been happy when he'd told her. She was one of the willing ones. She was addicted the same way he'd be, in five year's time. It was Jack's first brush with hard-core addiction, and he didn't realize you couldn't save someone who went down the rabbit hole willingly.

He didn't smarten up until Fiona tried to work a ritual on the sly as she writhed on top of him that left Jack choking and drained and near dead.

They'd had a row, and Fiona had left with a blackened eye and Jack with a rash of ruddy red nail marks down his cheek. And he hadn't seen her again. Never forgotten, though. Out of sight was not bloody out of mind, not where a girl like Fiona was concerned.

She seemed so different now. The cozy flat, the healthy flush and curve to her hips and breasts, the hair frizzy and natural, the tattoos she'd worn like brands faded away, no doubt hidden under demure necklines and high-waisted jeans when she'd gone out to the shops or to work.

Different, and dead. Fiona had cleaned up her act. They weren't supposed to get to you when you changed your wicked ways.

Jack yanked his hand back to his side. He was cold all over, all at once, his skin prickling like it had outside the flat, and he gazed around the room quickly, feeling his own talent spike in reaction to whatever he'd touched.

Just the last hint of Fiona's killer, the powerful and as-yet unknowable thing that could walk through walls and lock doors behind itself.

"I'm coming for you," Jack murmured. It hadn't been a bright idea to save Fiona the last time, and he wagered it was an even worse one this time around, but still, someone had murdered a girl he'd cared for once and there was something, as a mage, he could do about it to make sure they were never, ever able to hurt anyone again. "You mark the calendar, you cunt. I'm coming."

four

PETE waited until they were in the car park before she spoke. "How serious was it? With her?"

Her face was carefully closed, the neutral cop expression in play. Jack gauged his chances of being slapped, and then decided he was too tired for anything but the truth. "Unpleasantly serious at times."

Pete nodded, chewing that over. She wasn't a jealous woman, nor a petty one, but Jack knew if their situations were reversed he'd be wanting to find the nearest necromancer and bring Fiona Hannigan back so he could slap her in the teeth. "So can you tell Ollie what killed her?" Pete asked finally.

Jack sighed. "Maybe, with a little more digging. I'd like to get a look at her effects."

Pete frowned. "That'll be tough. They're evidence, and Ollie's not told his bosses about this little arrangement the two of you cooked up."

"Look," Jack said. "Heath pulled me into this. Ain't my problem if he's ashamed to admit he's consulting the wacky psychic bloke what lives down the lane instead of doing his job and detectiveing."

"Ollie isn't used to all this," Pete protested. "Hell, you remember what I was like when you first showed back up in my life? I'd've sooner believed in the tooth fairy than in most of the shite you take for granted."

Jack lifted his shoulder. "You handled it a lot better than Heath, trust me." She hadn't taken it in stride—no one who didn't grow up with a talent did—but Pete had faced up and faced the Black and she hadn't tried to deny what she saw at every turn.

"Speaking of," Pete said. "You need something, Ollie?" She walked over to where Heath was standing next to his car, red-faced.

Heath hit the window of the Vauxhall with the side of his fist. "Left my fucking keys in the ignition."

Jack saw a chance to get on Heath's good side—as good a side as Heath had, anyway. Helping out the police in their time of need was anathema to the way anyone like him lived, but if he wanted a look at Fiona's things, this was the easiest way.

"Let me," he said, shoving Ollie aside. Lock picking was fairly simple, as far as magic went, and it was the first charm a lot of mages bound for the shady side of the street taught themselves. Jack had taken to it quickly as any larcenous youngster, but there was more to it than slipping padlocks on storage warehouses, or deadbolts on back doors in neighborhoods where people actually had things worth nicking. Jack had an affinity for the locks, just as they responded to his touch like eager virgins. He wagered there wasn't much out there he couldn't break into, with a little skill and enough time.

Cars with computerized door locks made things a bit harder, but he still passed his hand across the door, and with a word and a breath and a shove of power the button popped up and the door sprang open. The alarm began whooping, and Heath scrambled for his keyring to shut it off.

"All right," he said, a frown furrowing his plump cheeks. "I admit. That was pretty good."

"Glad you were entertained," Jack said. "It occurs to me a fair trade would be a look at Fiona Hannigan's effects. The stuff on her when your ME took her off and sliced her open."

Heath started to say no, but Pete spoke up. "Ollie. If you want him to do the work, give him the tools."

Ollie relented, grumbling. "Fine, but we'll have to do it at your place. DCI Newell is going to be slagged beyond belief if he catches wind either of you are near this case."

"Brilliant," Jack said. "Come over and I'll put some tea on. Just for you."

five

HEATH didn't show up until after Jack and Pete had eaten supper, and he glanced comically from side to side before darting inside their flat. "I have to put these back in evidence before the morning shift comes in," he said, dropping a cardboard box on the sofa. "Be quick."

Pete looked at Jack. "Well, go to it," she said. "Show Ollie this wasn't a terrible fucking idea after all."

Jack flipped the lid off the box and shot her a dirty look. "Your faith in me is touching, luv."

She shrugged at him, and grinned as she lit a fag. Pete was slender but her lips were plump and made for sin, like a *femme fatale* at the cinema. She winked at him before she went into the kitchen, rattling the electric kettle. "Tea, Ollie?"

"Yes, please…" he murmured, staring at Jack's bookshelves. "Jesus Christmas, Winter. You really do live the dream, don't you?" He reached out and tapped at the preserved head in the jar of cloudy formaldehyde Jack used to prop up one end of his hex books, demonic keys and non-fiction.

"Oi," Jack said. "Leave Kevin alone."

Heath gawped. "It...it's alive?"

"Of course not," Jack sighed. "What do you take me for, a necromancer? It's a bloody severed head. And *its* name is Kevin." He grinned when he saw Heath wince and back away. Served him right for being a nosy bugger.

"Do you take sugar?" Pete asked pointedly, drawing Ollie into the kitchen. She glared at Jack over Heath's stooped shoulder and he spread his hands, hoping he looked innocent enough. Pete'd worked with Ollie for four years, and bloody well knew how he took his tea. She was just telling Jack to leave off being a wanker.

It was a hard impulse to resist in front of a detective inspector, but Jack wanted to see Fiona's things more than he wanted to wind Heath up. He lit a Parliament and settled with the box.

Fiona's wallet, a small quilted pouch that tied with a drawstring, yielded an Irish driver's license and seven quid, a receipt from a newsagent's and some lint. Her trouser pockets were empty of anything except a few stray sticks of nicotine gum.

She'd been trying to quit smoking. Jack exhaled a cloud of blue and looked through her purse. It was a knockoff, he supposed, all stiff leather and crookedly printed lining. His neighbors on the street probably sold one exactly like it. Jack tossed it aside. He wasn't interested in Fiona's fashion taste, or lack thereof. Not her mobile, encased neatly in a plastic evidence bag. Not the loose change and tampons and ancient tube schedule that peopled the bottom layer of the woman's most personal effects.

His fingers stopped on a small leather bag, barely bigger than a locket. "Hey Heath," he called. "You got any theories on what this is?"

Ollie craned his neck from the kitchen. "More of your bloody stuff, I'd imagine. Looks like something you'd wear to dress up and pretend to be vampires, you ask me."

Jack rolled the small bag between his fingers. You ran into real black magic, magic like Chester's, less often that one might think. Sorcerers were secretive, and they didn't appreciate every wank receptacle with a lip ring and a purple fauxhawk poking into their business. Most of what Jack had seen in his day were inept demon summonings, failed attempts at blood conjuring and a lot of poor, sad, dead Goths who bit off much more than their tortured souls could stomach.

But this was different. Holding it felt as if he held a dead bird. Limp and slimy, strands of vile power crawling all over his hand and arm. There wasn't much juice left in the little ball of spellcraft, but there was enough to get a sense of what it had been. Not the thing in Fiona's apartment, but a smaller, weaker approximation of it. A lure, made to hold the thing in place like a brook trout on a hook.

Jack gingerly untied the strings and let the piece of leather fall open. A small pinch of white powder that gave off the sweet, papery scent of a hothouse flower. A crow's feather, something snatched from Jack's own tradition. A silver coin, hand-stamped and green with age.

As Jack watched, everything in his palm began to burn and crumple, the maker of the bag no longer holding it together with her power.

Fiona's power. Fiona had made this thing, this dead-weight abomination that even now was making Jack's head ache and guts roil. This thing he wished he didn't recognize, but did, all too well.

Soon, Jack was holding nothing but a palmful of ash.

Pete's touch on his shoulder made it shift and fall, a black flutter of snow across the rug, and then nothing as even that faded away.

"I'm done," he told Pete. "I know what she was doing."

Pete took the things he'd scattered across the sofa and the floor, and packed them neatly back into the evidence box. She gave it to Ollie and said goodbyes.

Heath looked back at him. Jack watched smoke curl up from the end of his fag. "Winter," Heath said. "You'll be in touch, yeah?"

"As soon as he has anything you can use," Pete promised.

Heath remained, shuffling his feet in his infernal hard copper shoes. "Can you figure it out, Jack? This helped?"

"No," Jack said, stabbing his fag out viciously in the ashtray. "It did not bloody help me, Heath." Anger was always the best way to cover a lie. What he had to say wouldn't be of any use to Heath. Wouldn't help with his bloody closure. No one wants to hear their daughter or sister is mucking about with the forces of darkness.

"But it was useful," Pete was quick to amend. "I know we can work this for you, Ollie. You take care."

Jack stayed still for a long while after the door shut. Pete sat next to him. First her weight, and then her hand on his leg. "What?" she said. "I know that look. What?"

"I really thought she'd stopped all that," Jack said. He realized how fucking stupid he sounded as he voiced the thought. Like a teenage boy who really thought a pretty girl fancied him, zits and all. Right then, he was at the point where her boyfriend appeared and knocked the shite out of him for a fucking laugh.

"Sorcery?" Pete said. She took her hand away, and he heard the snap of her lighter and her deep inhale. "What was that thing, Jack?"

He got up and got himself a shot of whiskey in a juice glass, swallowed it down, and then went to the window. It was dark outside, but not dark enough yet for streetlamps. Everything was slate blue gray, like a bad memory. "A binding bag," he said. "For binding a spirit to you. It's the bastard child of the necromancer trick, you know...with the actual body." He breathed and his breath on the glass made the street below disappear. "This is more refined. Just for the soul."

"That sounds fairly unpleasant," Pete said. She went and got her laptop, settling herself back on the sofa.

"It's black magic," Jack said. "It's supposed to be un-fucking-pleasant." Fiona, binding ghosts. You could do all sorts of things with a ghost. None of them were for the continued good health of the person you were aiming it at. "Fuck," he said. He turned back to Pete. "I just thought she'd quit being that kind of girl."

"I'm sure," Pete said placidly. She didn't look irritated with him, or even angry, just sad. "But you know something, Jack?"

He sighed. "Fucking what?"

"You're not that kind of bloke any more." She came over to him and put a hand on his face. Her touch was like scalding water, but it drove away the last vestiges of Fiona's magic. Pete drew his face down so he had to look her in the eye. "Let's figure out who killed this silly woman and go back to regular life, yeah?"

Jack yanked a grimoire made of old notebook pages sewed together with red thread from between a paperback copy of *The Tell-Tale Heart* and a back issue of *Hustler*. "Yeah, okay."

Pete nodded. She never stayed sad for long. "So, ghost binding. Tell me what to look for."

"You're going to physically bind a ghost," Jack said. "You need some serious shit. Not just a bit of chalk and salt but the kind of stuff you can't just nip across the street to the Asian market for. Stuff not of this earth."

The pages of the grimoire stuck together, the blood that had seeped into the pages after its owner had taken two large-caliber slugs to the chest rusty with age. Jack hadn't been sorry that Parnell Grimes, Trish's dad and the ghost binder who'd owned the thing, had been shot, but he had been a bit sorry he wasn't the one to do it.

Parnell Grimes, in spite of being a fucking twat who delighted in human suffering almost as much as he delighted in torturing the dead, knew his stuff. Jack ran his finger down the partially destroyed list of ritual materials in the back of the book.

"Nightsong orchid," he said. Pete crinkled her nose.

"Sounds like a Goth band."

"It's a black flower that only blooms in the dark of the moon," Jack said. "Got a tiny throat and tongue that can sing you a song that'll send you into a poison sleep for a hundred years. Fae plant. You can only get it in the borderlands."

Anyone who'd risk messing about with the Fae to procure a few flowers was a serious sort indeed. Never mind the skill necessary to counteract the orchid's natural defenses so you didn't succumb to its charms, only to wake in the age of flying cars and a London ruled over by horny six-eyed space lizards.

"So where would this ghost-binder get it?" Pete asked.

Jack rubbed his chin. He needed a shave. He needed to sleep, to drink Fiona Hannigan's dead face out of his dreams. Instead he stood up, shoved his feet into his boots and got his leather.

"Only one place in London."

six

PEOPLE who talked about Hell on Earth, Jack decided, had never been to Peckham. Peckham echoed the ghost of an older London, one skinny and bleeding, with teeth out of its head, Thatcher in power, half the population drunk, out of work and pissing in the gutter. There was graffiti here, crime, dirt, and the howls of the city.

Jack walked down a small lane off the main road, reading the wall tags to pass the time. A few badly punctuated BNP propaganda phrases, gang tags, an attempt at artfulness across one of the storefront that showed a cluster of giant eyes staring down at passersby as they floated on a murky blue-black sea of stars and flowers.

He hunched into his collar, power crawling up and down his spine, and walked on. This close to the bone, magic felt like electricity on the skin, and Jack was holding his close, keeping it ready, like curling up your fist and putting weight on the balls of your feet.

The trick in bad neighborhoods was to behave as if you didn't give a fuck. Skinny white bloke walking alone through a known area of rough trade in fading twilight? Fuck it. Walk as if you're on Oxford Street at noon. Walk as if you haven't a fucking care in the world. There's only two reasons a bloke not working a corner walks down streets like this—looking to cop or looking for trouble. If you look as if you're relaxed and happy, having a bit of a stroll, people will assume you're a crazy arsehole who'll bite their faces off and make earrings from their nipples at the slightest provocation, and leave you the fuck alone.

Gemma's flat occupied the top floor of an old recording studio, back when singers with too much money and too much blow in their systems thought their shit synth-and-autotune records would sound more authentic recorded in London's arsehole. Gemma had converted the soundproofed rooms into just the sort of place she favored for doing business, and even in times such as these, Gemma's business was always good.

Jack noticed that the hex over the door was painted fresh, a little blood still sliding down the brick and to the sidewalk in fat black-wine drops.

He hit the buzzer and waited.

Gemma was very security conscious—Jack knew he'd be on video, and looked up at the small wireless camera bolted to the door frame, giving it a two-fingered salute. Gemma also had a sense of humor, when she was in her better moods. If her mood was foul, Jack could well find himself on the wrong end of a load of buckshot before he'd even said hello.

He hit the buzzer again, and finally the old-style security window in the door slid open with a clang. "WHAT."

the curse of FOUR

"And a fine evening to you too, guv," Jack said to the narrowed eyes and surly snarl on the other side of the steel door. "Gemma in?"

"Who the fuck's asking?" The voice was pure uncut London, but the face that Jack could see was sporting some impressive tattooing, ink faded and ragged at the edges. Prison ink, as if Gemma would employ anything less than the scariest bloody ex-con she could find. She probably thought having a mouth-breather like this shambling around making her clientele piss themselves was hilarious.

"Jack Winter," Jack said, getting up close and personal with the door slit. He felt a little of his power seep into his eyes, burning off with that ethereal, glowing blue that witchfire made. "Now open this door before I come through it and kick you in the balls for my trouble."

The goon snorted. "Not very polite, are you?"

Jack conjured a lit cigarette and sucked on it. "Getting less polite by the second."

A great many deadbolts and chains rattled on the other side of the door, and then the goon said "Do come in," with exaggerated ceremony. No doubt it was the code phrase to tag Jack as "friend" to that blacker-than-black hex above the door, rather than "food" or "now show me on the doll where the bad man touched you."

"Cheers," Jack said. Gemma had gotten new locks since he'd last been around, lo these many months. A top-end nine-pin number, the kind of thing paranoid kingpins stuck on their penthouse apartments to keep rival dealers out. And her butler was both larger and dumber than old Hakim, who'd really been pretty decent, for a pusher's muscle, and big fan of Jack's band.

"I'll tell her you're here," said the new muscle, and started ham-fistedly poking the call box like an enthusiastic but inexperienced teenager on a date. Jack got a better look at him. Huge, shirtless, tattooed everywhere visible and likely a few places Jack didn't want to imagine.

There was something about the bloke—it wasn't that he was big enough to turn normal-sized human heads into bowling balls, not his shaved skull, not his parade of earrings and facial piercings. He didn't smell right, didn't register on Jack's scale of *human* to *what the fuck is that??* properly.

Jack's forehead started a small ache, his sight showing him stringy rotted muscle, skin gone green with bloat and decay.

"Fuck me and your sister," Jack said, just as Gemma came floating regally down the crumbling, piss-stained stairway. "Gemma, when the fuck did you start hiring zombies?"

"When having a live man on the door ceased to be cost-effective," Gemma said. She took Jack by the chin, turned his face this way and that. "Look at you, as I live and breathe."

She pivoted on one heel of fine calfskin boots hugging fine, shapely calves and beckoned him up the stairs. The zombie slumped back to a stool by the door and picked up a dog-eared *Hello!* Zombies couldn't generally read. Maybe he liked the pictures.

The upper half of the recording studio was opened up into a flat, filled with long low leather sofas, chrome tables, a rug made from the hide of something red and cow-sized. There were photographs on the walls of slender naked women in improbable poses, some slick modern art, an open kitchen devoid of food or plates. Jack had always wagered that if Gemma cared about sex, she was probably a lesbian, but he knew she didn't stoop to such pursuits. Gemma loved trade. Cold hard cash made her hot. The bargain, getting the upper hand via a person's desperation. Drug dealers and demons had that in common.

"Well, here's a sight I thought I'd never fucking see," Gemma purred, going to a lacquered Chinese cabinet made into a bar and pouring something into a heavy tumbler. Jack tasted it when she set it into his hand. Whiskey, smooth and hot and expensive. Gemma knew every client's every vice.

"What's that?" he said after the first swallow had gone down.

"Jack Winter sitting on my sofa," Gemma replied, mixing her own drink. Tonic water and a twist. Gemma didn't drink, have sex or smoke. She was a bit like an evil nun. Her perfect red lips didn't even leave a smudge mark on her tumbler. "Thought you'd straightened up and flown right, and were far too good for the likes of me."

Jack tipped his eyebrow up. "Now you know I'd never think that, Gemma."

Gemma was, he supposed, a beautiful woman by most standards. Pale ashy blond hair, light eyes, cut-glass bone structure and not enough weight to keep her from blowing away in a high wind. But if you really looked, Gemma was hollow. She was glass, filled up with sand. Jack wouldn't turn his back on her, not on his best day.

"I always did like you," Gemma said. "You were like a sad puppy. I couldn't help myself." She eyed him up and down. "But you're clean. I suppose you've got no more use for me."

"I've kicked," Jack admitted. "About four months now."

"How lovely," Gemma said dryly. "And I'm sure you found some sweet little thing to hold your hair back while you were vomiting yourself toward moral uprightness. Is she a sucker for men who shoot smack because she can fix them like she couldn't fix Daddy, or does she simply get off on lost causes?"

Jack ignored the venom. That was just part and parcel of Gemma. He'd been a good customer, and Pete had taken him away. Simple. "Neither," he said. "She handcuffed me to a bed until it was out of me system. I think she brought me an aspirin once."

Gemma let out a genuine laugh. "Perhaps I was hasty. Sounds as if I'd like her."

"Listen," Jack said, knowing she was stroking him as a former client, and perhaps a current one, and not liking the memory it brought up. "I do have something to ask you about."

Gemma had mixed his whiskey with tea when he'd come to her before, because he was constantly shivering. Twenty pounds lighter, he couldn't keep any heat next to his skin even if he wanted to. She'd always offered him biscuits or a sandwich as well, even though he was never hungry. Pushed his sweaty, grimy hair out of his face and offered him a few pounds to take a cab back to wherever his squat of the moment was. Once, she'd just taken a crop of men's couture in trade from a mage client, and she gave him an Armani overcoat worth as much as a month's rent on his flat. Jack had never worn it—wearing something like that was just asking for a blade in your kidney, with the sort of people he normally went around with, but it had traded for a week's worth of hits to a flash Jamaican git named Corley.

Life was so simple then. Sick, dirty and simple.

"Ask away, love," Gemma said. "Can't promise I'll answer." She sucked the pulp from her lemon twist, small square white teeth working industriously.

Jack drained his tumbler and stood, rolling it in his hands. "Had much call for nightsong orchids lately?" He watched Gemma as he said it, and was rewarded. She twitched.

"I'm an entrepreneur, not a fucking florist," was her reply, said with a toss of her golden head and half a second too late. She jostled the ice in her empty glass, as a snake would shake its rattle.

"Gemma." Jack tilted his head at her. "I'm a junkie bum, it's true, but 'm not a fucking idiot."

Her porcelain expression dropped for just a moment and her eyes flicked from side to side. "Why are you coming back asking questions *now*, Jack? Why fucking now? Always had the worst bloody timing, didn't you?"

Jack went to her, put his hands on her shoulders. "Who's giving you trouble, Gem? I saw the lock. I'm assuming Hakim got himself all filled full of dead and you replaced him with that hunk of meat down there. What's going on?"

Gemma had kept him in smack, yes, but she wasn't a bad sort, as far as those things went.

"It's a bloke came 'round about six months ago," Gemma said. "It's odd, but I couldn't tell you anything about him now if you ran a current through me. Anyway, he said I could pay him or get out."

"And?" Jack knew that Gemma's style wasn't to pay protection money to anyone, man, demon or Other.

"I told him to go jam his little extortion scheme up his arse, of course, and hold it there for a good long while," Gemma said. "Next day, Hakim is on my doorstep with half of his fucking face missing. Week after that, they broke into my flat and did a real number on the place. Standard stuff, but....they were in my *flat,* Jack. Never saw that bloke again—it's been a gang of Turks he has running for him doing the sordid business." She sniffed. "Hakim didn't deserve that."

Jack turned the story over in his mind. A lot of things could make you forget—spells, rituals, charms, or something as mundane as a GHB chaser in your non-cocktail. But Jack was betting with the sort of clientele Gemma saw, it was magic.

"Somebody interested in your business?" he said. "Same somebody buying nightsong orchids?"

"*That* fuckwit," Gemma spat. "Never. He's a moron." She blushed, realizing she'd told Jack exactly what he needed. "Look, I don't know the bloke. He set it up through one of my regulars down at Memento Mori."

"That nancy club in the Docklands?" Jack blinked in surprise. "Thought you wouldn't touch that place with a ten-foot pole."

Gemma ducked out from under his arms and walked into her back room, which was a hallucinatory combination of storeroom, apothecary, gun safe, antique shop and chemistry lab gone wrong. Bundles of less rare herbs hung from the ceiling, neat shelves paraded this way and that groaning with grimoires and artifacts, and a huge, ancient safe at one end of the room, done up with protection hexes and bindings in neat strokes, held the real juicy stuff. Gemma had shown him once, when she was in an expansive mood. Some of the things in the safe could have leveled greater

London, and some were so bad Jack only got a glimpse before his sight came screaming through his smack haze with a flash flood of nightmares and landscapes beyond anything he'd ever witnessed.

He'd gotten absolutely fucking wasted that night, in a doorway around the corner from Gemma's flat, until he'd mostly erased what he'd seen. But he'd never forgotten the lesson inherent in Gemma's showing off—she wasn't to be fucked with in any way, shape or form.

On a table by the window were flowers and living things in bell jars, small terrariums for rare frogs and insects from Hell, Faerie and a thousand places in between, as well as endangered or forgotten but thoroughly terrestrial plants that Gemma sold to the nicer sort of witches that came to her door.

Gemma laid her hand on the largest of the jars, containing a single plant in rich brown earth. The nightsong orchid's throat worked, weaving its seduction song, trying to lull Gemma to sleep. Jack felt a dull throb at the base of his skull as the Black vibrated around the vile thing. Three flowers were blooming, blacker than a sky and softer than innocent skin.

"These go for five thousand quid apiece," Gemma said. "I have to wear specially made headphones to harvest the fucking thing, and it gives me a rash. So yes, I do trade with my mystery man at the club. It's worth my time."

"Thank you, luv," Jack said sincerely. "I should be going."

"Here." Gemma pulled a small baggie from one of the apothecary drawers that went floor to ceiling along one wall. "Have some. For old time's sake."

Jack tucked it into his pocket, nodded at Gemma. "I can let myself out."

"Jack." He was almost to the door, but he turned around.

"Be careful," Gemma said. "Whoever's using nightsong orchid besides my client—they're not a bloke I'd fuck with. That plus all of this unrest, another mage pushing in on my operation—there's some heavy fucking power flowing right now, and knowing you you're going to stick your nose in it like a stupid kid sticks his hand in a torch flame."

"You do know me well," Jack said.

"I do," Gemma said as she shut the door. "That's the problem."

In the street, on his way back to the tube, he took out the small plastic bag, neatly sealed and labeled. Gemma was meticulous in all things. He had no use for nightsong orchid, but the fact that Gemma had given him a gift made him smile. Still, she could have given him something useful, like graveyard dirt or inferno weed.

Inferno weed was the kudzu vine of Hell, a creeping parasite that burned hotter than thermite. Jack had used his last bit disposing of a horde of sorcerers who'd broken into his flat and tried to install the ghost of their master into Jack's body, without Jack's consent.

Algernon Treadwell. What a fucking nonce he'd been.

That had been the first time Jack had heard of binding a ghost to a living body. The first time he'd known such a thing, such a terrifying, vile thing, was possible. And now it looked like at least Fiona had tried the same thing, tried and gotten her blood spattered across her own flat for her trouble.

Who the fuck would want a ghost sharing breathing space? What the fuck could they possibly be getting out of it?

Fiona, what the fuck did you get yourself into?

seven

MEMENTO Mori was impressed enough with itself that it didn't open until ten p.m., so Jack spent the next day clearing the backlog of work Pete always pestered him to do and he avoided studiously as the plague. She'd also been quiet and grim since the scene with Fiona's body, and he felt he owned it to her not to be an utter fucking twat for a few hours.

"Demonic possession in Shropshire," Pete said, scrolling through the mailbox she'd set up for her and Jack's business matters.

"Bloody hell, no," Jack said. "Send it to Mickey Grant. Sounds about his speed, and he always loved those country girls with thick ankles."

Pete tossed a wad of paper at his head. "You know, you could come and look through these yourself."

Jack snorted. "Why, when I get to hear your dulcet tones?"

"Poltergeist in the Royal Albert Hall," Pete read. Jack put an arm over his eyes.

"No."

"Haunting at the Glastonbury police station."

"*Fuck* no."

Pete sighed, and Jack knew he was going to have to pick something soon, before she threw a more substantial object at his head. "Oh," she said, and then, "Listen to this."

Jack sat up and listened. All he'd been doing was thinking about Fiona and the two other murders anyway. Wondering if he could grease up his rusty manipulation charms enough to talk Heath into letting him look at the case notes. Nothing useful.

"It's a man from *Cellar* magazine," Pete said. "You know, *Cellar*—I used to read it when I was in school." Pete had been a crusty punk's wet dream in those days—a Catholic school uniform topped by spiky Joan Jett hair, too much eyeliner, and a snarl.

Jack tried to banish the indecent ideas the memory conjured, at least enough to listen to Pete. "Yeah, *Cellar*—that fucking rag still about?" *Cellar* had only had one mention of the Poor Dead Bastards, *Like dying goats being sodomized by the bastard children of GG Allin and a howler monkey (no pun intended).*

"About, and this fellow wants to interview you," Pete said. "Some retrospective thing. Seems you're the only Bastard he's been able to find."

"Tell him to sod off," Jack said, and lay back down, replacing his arm over his face. Keys clicked, and Jack cracked an eye open. "What are you saying?"

"That you can meet him this afternoon," Pete said. "And that you're very excited."

Jack shook his head. "You're an evil woman, you know? A bane on my very existence."

"Of course I am," Pete said. "Why else would I hang around with you?"

eight

THE man from *Cellar*—sounded like it should be a cheaply shot BBC spy programmed, of 1970s vintage, Jack thought—met him in the White Hart pub down the street from Jack's flat. The White Hart had a few live shows still, not-half-bad neo-punk stuff that would be genuinely good in another few years. Jack was willing to bet the bloke found out about it from the internet.

"Matthew Killian," he said as soon as Jack sat down, extending his hand. Jack decided to shake it, see what he could pick up. Nervousness, a little something speeding through Matthew Killian's bloodstream—prescribed pseudo-legally, no doubt. Matthew didn't look old enough to remember coke, but the strongest vibration he emitted was pure, reeking insincerity.

In other words, your standard-issue music journalist.

"And you're Jack Winter," Killian said. To his credit, he wasn't actually wearing thick-rimmed black glasses or something genuinely offensive, like a vintage Dead Kennedys shirt older than his person, but the black denim, unlaced army boots and mussed dyed-black hair were enough. Killian was too sharp-looking, too pretty to be anything but some West End nonce who'd run away from his trust fund and his daddy issues to play with the punks.

"Right in one," Jack said. Killian set a digital recorder on the table.

"Hope that's all right. Can I get you anything before we start?"

"Coffee," Jack said, and picked up a glare from the shaven-headed, tattooed Pakistani publican leaning on the bar. Yusef knew him well enough, but he clearly didn't like Killian any more than Jack did.

Killian practically scrambled up and came back with a coffee. Jack uncapped his flask and filled the mug to the rim with whiskey, then took a few hot, sour gulps. "You going to ask me something, or stare at me like me knob's hanging out until it's time for you to catch the train?" Jack demanded.

Killian grinned as if Jack had bestowed the secret password to Hell and Heaven (if there had actually been such a place as Heaven) upon him. "Shit, man. You haven't changed at all."

"Old enough to have seen a show, are you?" Jack said, feeling his eyebrows attempt to crawl away into his hair from sheer skepticism.

"No, but I have your LP and a I've written a lot about you. The Bastards are sort of my pet project."

"Really." Jack finished off his coffee. "How nice. I'm partial to scrap booking and collecting tea cozies, meself."

"Let me just go over what I know, yeah?" Killian said. "The Bastards formed in '88...original lineup all the way through, consisting of you, Dix McGowan, Richard Whitehall, and Gavin Lecroix. Released one LP on a miniscule DIY label, circa 1993 and a handful of singles before and after. *Nightmares and Strange Days* well-received by critics but considered a bit too strange, a bit too Nick Cave, if you will, for the boots-and-bristle cut set. Lots of dark imagery, angels and demons and all that shit—not that it's shit. You drop off the grid in '96 after a few years of, pardon my French, increasingly fucking odd behavior, and with a twelve year gap of mystery...here you are."

Jack had to give Killian credit—the little bastard wasn't shy around his idols. He got a cigarette the usual way and lit it with a thought. If Killian noticed, he didn't mention it.

"Can I ask where you went?" Killian said. He leaned across the table. "There are a couple of popular theories among your fans. You got pinched. You signed an enormous record deal in America to do a grunge album under another name. While I don't doubt that fine end-stage Billy Idol growl you've got would suit, my personal theory is it was a woman. You always did have a taste for young and juicy tail, according to everyone who knows you." The twat actually pushed the recorder closer to Jack. "So what happened? I'm right, aren't I?"

"Yeah," Jack said. "I was off having an extended threesome with lady smack and her sister self-pity. Regular pair of needy sluts, those two—they'll do absolutely anything to keep you around."

Killian sat back, his lips opening. Jack smirked, stubbing out his cigarette. That had shut him up.

"If that's the question you came to ask," Jack said, standing. "Then I have a real life to get back to. That one was shit. I'm well rid of it." It wasn't entirely true. Being a musician had been a hell of a lot easier than being a mage, and kinder to his back, his knees and his sanity.

"Wait!" Killian squeaked. Jack turned back.

"Yes?"

"Tell me," Killian said, fumbling in his jeans for a wad of bills. He put them on the table. "I'll buy you as much shitty coffee as you need, but you have to tell me. You have to tell me... what happened. Where you disappeared to."

I thought I was the wickedest man in the world, Jack wanted to say. *And a hungry ghost showed me the error of me fucking ways.*

Jack sat down again. Yusef came around the bar and gave him a fresh cup of coffee along with the eyebrow lift, heavy with rings, that asked, *You want me to kick this tosser's arse?* Jack shook his head. "Cheers, Yusef." He put his attention back on Killian. "I see one fucking word of this in print, I'm coming down to your eco-friendly, sustainable produce, no-dress-code open-plan poncey little office and pulling your jawbone backwards through your arse. Got it?"

Killian blinked once, his throat tightened. "Got it," he whispered. Jack was glad to see that he at least hadn't lost his ability to scare the piss out of pushy little children with delusions of importance.

"Tell me," Killian said, voice regaining a little of its surety. "I want to know."

Jack sighed, lit another fag, poisoned the air around him with a blue cloud that was a pale imitation of his witchfire. "I met a girl."

nine

MEETING Pete was just the final nail in the coffin, of course. Things had been sideways for a long time before she walked into his life, a vision in Siouxsie eyeliner and a shredded school uniform.

Rich, his guitarist, was getting shite from his girlfriend about her still being a girlfriend and not a wife. The usual grow up and get a real job speech most women gave at some point, except Rich bought it. Dix—far and away the best musician in the band, Jack freely admitted, because it sure as fuck wasn't him—was getting more and more offers of gigging with more serious outfits who drank less, practiced more and didn't have a frontman with one foot in a world that should be relegated to a fairy story.

And this was after Fiona, after he'd gone down her particular rabbit hole of great bloody sex and even greater bloody problems. Getting Fiona clean had been his project, more than the band. Everyone except Gavin had pretty much stopped speaking to him when he finally gave up and let Fiona go back to Chester and his little group of mage-fuckers.

Gavin was the only one who didn't give Jack shit about his magic. Gavin wanted to learn, even though he didn't have a talent, wanted to understand. Jack was just grateful there was one person on earth who didn't think he was a complete twat.

And then Pete had appeared, with her strange, wild magic that got his blood moving like nothing had in years. Theoretically, Jack had been dating her chestier, more age-appropriate sister, but Pete had put that notion right out of his head. She had a way of touching him, of seeing into him, that was like putting his hands in fire and coming away unscathed. He couldn't think of anything but Pete, and when they weren't sleeping together in his filthy bedsit that he'd moved into on the sly, he was thinking of ways to show her exactly what his world was, and what she could be if she came to live in it.

Jack freely admitted it—he got bent over and screwed because he was trying to impress his fucking girlfriend.

Treadwell had come, had tried to rob him of his body and his life, and though Jack had put him back, Pete had run away and had never come back.

As any sensible girl would do. And even though she was sixteen, sneaking out to clubs, and doing unspeakable things to a musician twice her age, Pete was, even then, a lot more fucking sensible than he was.

"I fucked up," Jack finished, having told Killian most of it and leaving out the magic. "That good enough for your rag?"

Killian blinked, as if he were coming out of a trance. "Brilliant."

"Yeah," Jack said, hoping his sarcasm was evident. "Bloody brilliant, right? Absolutely tip-top."

The Bastards had kicked him out and broken apart virtually in the same week, Rich moving in with his girlfriend and her parents and buying a cheap ring, Dix taking a job as a studio drummer for Virgin Records, and Gavin drifting back to wherever Gavin had come from. Jack regretted that. Out of all his band mates, Gavin was the one who had turned into the least insufferable cunt.

"That enough? We done?" Jack asked Killian. Killian nodded, scrambling to gather up his tape and notes.

"I got what I needed, yeah."

"Good." Jack shoved back his chair and stood up. "'Cause I've got real work to do."

ten

MEMENTO Mori occupied a warehouse space in the Docklands, which at one time had been one of the worst parts of London. Thanks to gentrification, overpopulation and the post-Thatcher push to bury the wicked old past, the Docklands now were largely a shining expanse jutting into the Thames, full of trendy shops and trendier nightclubs and, it seemed, a bastion of black magic that exuded malice like an infected wound exudes pus.

Jack stood across the street, under the awning of a boutique called Precious, which seemed to specialize in themed baby clothes. From the outside, the club looked like any other along the stretch. Subtle neon graced the window, a metal door with a porthole stood guard, and blacked out windows told the unwashed, un-beautiful masses they were not welcome. Even the bouncer standing by the door with a Bluetooth earpiece was tasteful.

You had to look past what the eye could discern to see the blot, the stain on the place. It was a halo of filth and pain that hovered like a crown of blowflies over a dead body. It shimmered the air under Jack's sight, distorted it like heatwaves. There was a powerful lot of bad juju in the air of Memento Mori, and Jack intended to go inside and find out who made it that way. Or what.

Stamping on his fag to put it out, Jack crossed the pedestrian walkway ahead of a flying V of German tourists, laughing loud, broad Teutonic laughs that exuded the scent of English beer. Drunk and grinning and blissfully unaware of the dank, evil building squatting just to their left, they rolled on, snapping pictures of one another pulling ludicrous faces. Jack envied them, the bratwurst-munching sods.

He stopped in front of the bouncer and jerked his head to get the man's attention. "Oi."

The bouncer looked him over, slowly. "You get lost on your way to the gutter, mate?"

"Clever," Jack said. "You think of that one all by yourself or did you get it off last night's Jonathan Ross?"

The bouncer folded forearms the width of Jack's neck. "All right, funny man. Cut the shit and tell me what you want."

"Not what I want," Jack said. "See, what I want's not the question. What I'm *doing* is going through that door, and the *question* is whether I do it around you or over you, while you're lying on the ground clutching what remains of both your dignity and your bollocks."

The bouncer jutted his chin, but his heartbeat picked up, veins beating under his thick skin. Jack didn't feel any prickle of power. Score one for his side—Memento Mori was cheap about its brute force help. The bouncer was only human—a fucking enormous, violence-inclined human, but non-magical none the less. If he'd had any hint of a talent, Jack would have been flying arse over teakettle into the Thames by now. And he'd have deserved it.

"What's your name?" he said after a minute.

"Jack Winter," Jack said. Sometimes his name still held a little currency, but not in places like this. Never places like this.

The bouncer looked off into space for a moment, touching his earpiece. Then, wonder of wonders, he moved his massive mountain-body aside and opened the door.

"Go right in, Mr. Winter. Seems all the fuss wasn't necessary."

Jack eyed him as he stepped gingerly to the threshold. No protection hexes ground against his sight, so he proceeded. "How's that?"

The bouncer gave him a humorless smirk. "They've been expecting you."

Before Jack could question either his luck or the invisible "They's" motive, the door slammed shut with the sound of a coffin or a deep-sea capsule, leaving him alone and in the dark.

Jack took a moment to let his eyes adjust. He was in a long hallway, only a neon blue cross, of the type you saw on churches in the deep American South, indicated a passage to the club itself. The heartbeat of bass made the walls throb and the floor hum under Jack's feet.

Whoever had given Fiona the nightsong orchid was here. Knew him. Wanted to see him.

Jack didn't like being the one in the dark, literally or figuratively, or both. He didn't like not knowing what he was walking into. Too often, you were walking into a fist in your teeth and waking up the next morning in some backwater gutter with pain in your head and empty pockets.

Still, he shoved his hands into his pockets and walked under the arch, into the noise and the crush.

Memento Mori was miles more posh than the clubs Jack had played in during his days with the Bastards. The walls hung heavy with midnight blue velvet drapes, and the booths were slick and black, tables of heavy blood-red wood supporting the drinks and elbows of the fashionably bored. Jack hadn't seen that many frilly cuffs and fluffy cravats since he'd first come to London in 1984. A band of thin, pale, androgynous figures gyrated onstage, moving as if the horrid, nonsensical house music the DJ droned into the PA were slowly melting their brains out their ears.

Someone touched his arm, and he turned to see a pale, pretty waitress strapped into leather shorts and a bondage top that barely bound in anything looking up at him. "Please come with me, Mr. Winter. My name is Amberleigh."

Even though the club was ear-bleedingly loud, Jack heard her perfectly. It was only a small trick, but he pulled his arm away. "Lead on, luv," was all he said. Amberleigh didn't have much of an effect on his sight—and many people only did have a small talent, more of a knack, but magic was magic and Jack had learned a long time ago not to turn his back on it.

Amberleigh wound among the dancers and her fellow waitresses, waterfall of black hair twitching in time with her arse. Jack looked—he was human, after all, last time he checked—but he paid more attention to the door she was taking him to.

Sanctum spelled out in more discreet neon.

the curse of FOUR

Amberleigh tapped twice on the door, and then led Jack inside. When the door slid shut, the noise died abruptly.

Jack cast a look around the room. Typical VIP suite to the naked eye—more of the velvet booths, more shiny liquor bottles behind a small black ebony bar staffed by another virtually topless woman fidgeting her lip ring with her tongue. Jack walked straight to her. "Whiskey, luv. Cheers."

"Piss off," the bartender said. Jack blinked and looked at Amberleigh.

"Mr. Waverly didn't ask you here to drink his liquor and be rude," she elaborated. Jack gave her a tight smile.

"You tell Mr. Waverly that unless he wants me in a worse fucking mood than I already am, to give me some god-damned social lubrication, please and thank you so very fucking much."

Amberleigh's wide, plump mouth scrunched up, but she turned and disappeared through a thin door set invisibly into the velvet walls—an office, Jack thought, probably the owner's.

He nodded to the bartender. "Nice tits. They come with the job?"

"Up yours, you fucking poof," she said, and retreated to the end of the bar.

Jack sighed and looked at the ceiling, where a nice, neat protection hex was chalked. To anyone not a mage it simply looked like more of the high-end Gothic décor running rampant through the rest of Memento Mori, but Jack knew better. A small animal paw was nailed to the crossbeam, surrounded with black thread and crowned with a spring of belladonna. The hex wouldn't just give anyone unwanted a friendly warning, it would strip the skin off your bones. Jack gave a sigh. Always nice to know who you were dealing with. So far Gemma's information had been accurate—black magic user and fucking tosser.

"Jack," Amberleigh said at his back, in that too-young voice. "This is Trent. Mr. Waverly, I mean."

"Mr. Winter." Trent Waverly was the type of man that Jack disliked on sight—sharply dressed, soft hands, a little pouch of fat under his jaw, black hair combed over his forehead and his ridiculous black velvet suit combining to give Jack the impression of no one so much as Anton LaVey's younger, fatter brother.

"This is quite the treat," Waverly said. "Hearing you dropped in will send business through the roof." He sat and adjusted his cuffs. "If I'd know you were interested, I would have sent you a car. You have a woman? Man? Bring them next time. Or we can arrange company here." He patted Amberleigh on the bottom and sent her on her way back to the main club.

"That's very kind of you, mate," Jack said as the door let in another snatch of vibrating bass, "but I don't think I remember the 80s as fondly as you do."

Waverly grimaced. "What the fuck do you want, then? Aside from coming here to waste my time?"

Jack did take the seat then, and got close enough to smell the cologne on Waverly's neck and see the dandruff of coke powder on his black lapels. "There's a girl came in here named Fiona Hannigan. You gave her something that got her killed."

Waverly snorted. "'Less she was on her knees sucking my cock as payment, I wouldn't know her from Eve. I'm not some drug dealer with a mobile and a fake gold chain, Mr. Winter. My clients are anonymous and I work hard to not learn names and faces."

Jack took out his flick knife, and very deliberately opened in under Waverly's nose. "I don't think I'm keen on you talking about Fiona that way, boyo."

Waverly rolled his eyes up at the ceiling. "You lay one finger on me and that hex will have its way with you, bent over and trousers down." He sniffed deeply, his abused sinus cavities lending his laugh a wet cast. "So have a drink and a laugh, Winter, or fuck off. Either way...the hard man act doesn't fly here."

Amberleigh, the waitress, appeared and set down a glass of whiskey at his elbow. "Your drink, Mr. Winter." She ran her fingers across the back of his neck. Sticky and red-hot, a memory of the sex magic Fiona had used to reel him in.

Jack grabbed up the glass, the decision coming over him without thinking at all. He was reaching back to the bloke he'd been when he was with Fiona, the hard bastard who made cunts like Trent Waverly get the fuck out of his way.

He tipped the whiskey out onto the floor and slammed the glass back down hard, smashing it into the table with the flat of his hand. The tumbler shattered, the largest shard slicing into Jack's palm. Jack grabbed Waverly by his shirt, pressing his bloody hand against the man's plump, quivering cheek.

"Fuck!" Waverly screamed. "Get the fuck off me, you tosser! I dunno where you've been!"

"Fiona fucking Hannigan," Jack snarled, grabbing Waverly by the jaw. His blood was pumping hard, anger driving his heart rate into the red zone, and it was all over Waverly, down into his collar and across his cheeks and mouth. Even a shite magician like Waverly knew there was power in blood, that being covered in it marked you as prey. Waverly struggled and choked, flailing his arms at the bartender, who watched the entire thing as if they were a particularly diverting episode of *Footballer's Wives.*

"I barely knew that stupid whore!" Waverly choked. "Oh Christ, it's in my *mouth...*"

"You think I'm afraid of your hexes now?" Jack shouted. "You think I give a fuck, Waverly? *What did you give her?*"

"Orchid! And some words!" Waverly shrieked. "She came in here looking for binding hexes and nightsong orchid! I took payment in trade!" He stopped moving and rolled his eyes to meet Jack's. "Oh fuck me—is she your girlfriend?"

Jack felt limp, suddenly, limp and lightheaded as blood dripped down his sleeve and warmed his skin. Fiona had done exactly what he thought she had. She was the same girl he'd left to her fate. And she was dead because of it.

He hadn't come back for her.

Jack let go of Waverly and stood up. "We're old news," he said.

"You...you *cunt,*" Waverly screamed as he started for the door. "I ever clap eyes on you again, you're fucking *wasted,* mate! You're fertilizer!"

Jack smeared his hand across the door before he opened it. "Looking forward to that," he said, and walked out. He stomped back to the bar in the club, and thumped on it with his fist. "Whiskey. Neat. And get me a towel." The bartender heaved an exaggerated sigh, his silk vest and shirt and his natty silver piercings in keeping with the rest of the poncey club. Jack looked him in the eye.

"You think I'm bad now, you don't want to see what'll happen you don't pour me a drink," he snarled.

the curse of FOUR

The boy thumped a glass in front of him and Jack tossed it back before he wrapped a bar towel around his hand. The cut was deep but small and clean. He wouldn't die from it. His good hand still shook as he set the empty glass down.

Fiona hadn't changed. She'd fallen into her old ways, trafficking with the kind of sods who rolled around in the mud pit with the worst the Black had to offer. But for what? Not for money or power, like with Chester's particular brand of fuckwittery. She'd lived like a student and whatever power she had wasn't enough to stop someone from slipping into the flat and killing her.

Or Waverly was lying his face off, one or the other. Jack supposed if he was being rational about this, he'd have Heath check Waverly out in the morning, bring the hammer of the Met down on Memento Mori, and let them sort it out.

Jack wasn't feeling particularly reasonable.

The fey bartender appeared and refilled his glass before he could yell again, so that was something. "Cut yourself shaving?" the bartender offered. Jack flipped him the bird in response.

He wasn't sure what happened after that. The music seemed to be inside his head, throbbing in time with his heartbeat. He could feel the crowd breathing, sweating, closing in around him. He felt the part of him that was his talent, that was inexorably linked to the Black, slide out of his grasp and go trickling away between his fingertips.

Jack thought he might have slid off his stool, and hit the floor—the throbbing in his head intensified, his vision a fractal of a million slices of red light and hot, white pain. He felt like he'd broken into a million pieces and scattered across the psychic spectrum. Someone screamed, or maybe it was just the caw of a crow, and then he was gone, down into the deepest ocean of dreaming.

eleven

JACK came awake all at once, mind and body, and the lurch of his nerves catapulted him off the soft surface cradling him and onto the floor. He landed on his side, hard, and his belt and his flick-knife drove into his side with twin boot-kicks of pain.

"Fuck!" he shouted. The dilapidated Moorish chandelier hanging from the ceiling of his flat rattled.

His flat. He was in his flat.

Jack dug his fingertips into his throbbing forehead. How the fuck had he gotten back to Whitechapel from the Docklands?

His memory was black and fuzzy after he'd tossed back that second whiskey. Third? He'd passed out. Hit his head.

Waverly. Had Waverly sent him home? Not likely, after he'd made pop art out of the man's face. Had Waverly done this to him, some passive-aggressive form of revenge for Jack getting into his personal space? That seemed a far bit more likely.

Jack rolled to his feet and shrugged out of his jacket, tossing it back on the sofa while he stumbled into the bathroom.

Enough blackouts and mornings after and you develop a routine—check for injuries. His hand was throbbing but it had stopped bleeding and the cut was starting to close over.

Right. Take inventory of your pockets. His wallet was still in evidence, and all the bits and scraps he collected throughout the days leading up to his visit with Waverly—vellum scratch paper, a nub of chalk for working out sigils and hexes on a hard surface, a ballpoint pen from the curry stand around the corner, a receipt from the off-license for a bottle of Jameson.

Fucking whiskey. He was going to have to give it up, sooner or later, just as Pete kept telling him they should both give up fags. Sooner or later he was going to end up tan and healthy and fucking respectable, whether he liked it or not.

Inventory of the self was next. Make sure all your fingers and toes are working, take account of the new bangs and bruises—Jack grimaced at the crust of blood and bruise on the side of his head, turning the short hairs at his temple pink instead of bottle blond. The bruise continued down the side of his face, staining his cheekbone blue.

Jack brought his fingers up to prod the head wound—he couldn't simply show up to A&E if he had a concussion, not with how his life worked—and then paused.

His good hand was red. Not "Ah shit, I've got some of my own blood on me" red. Dipped-in-paint, dried, caked-on red.

His shirt was red, when he looked down at himself. Smeared like some pretentious fuck's painting at the Tate.

Jack had seen enough blood to know what was on his skin, his shirt and his denim and his boots. He was smeared in the stuff, as if he'd fallen into it face first. Only his face was clean, and his leather when he strode back to the sitting room to check. That might explain how he'd made it home without respectable folk screaming and phoning the police.

He turned out his pockets, his flick-knife clattering to the floor. The blade, when he opened it, was stained dark blood-black. Fiona's key that he'd lifted from Ollie clattered out with it, onto the floor, but Jack ignored it.

It wasn't his blood. That much was certain.

There was far too much for it to be an animal, at least one of the size you'd typically find in metropolitan London.

So that left the question of who the blood belonged to, and how the fuck it had gotten all over him.

Before Jack could consider his options, pounding started up at the front door, in time with his head. "Jack Winter! Open this fucking door!"

Heath. Jack spit a curse under his breath, in one of the demonic dialects, that translated roughly into *may rabid cats fly up your arse.*

"I know you're in there, Winter!" Ollie bellowed. "I've got a uniform under your fire escape, and if you try anything dodgy I will personally put a pair of bullets in your clever little brain!"

Jack couldn't argue with logic like that. He shoved the flick knife down between the sofa cushions—because there was no point in looking like even more of a homicidal git than he already did—and went to the door, undoing the chain.

Ollie practically knocked him down coming in. The shorter man's color was up, and he brandished his pudgy index finger at Jack. "What the fuck is that all over you?"

"Catsup," Jack said. "Went a bit mad with me morning fry-up."

Ollie hit Jack, and he was surprised that the blow actually knocked him off balance enough to sit down hard, legs splayed. Of course, he excused it, he'd already had his bell rung by a floor and likely some kind of dose designed to make the previous night a blur.

"You keep up that smart-arse shite," Ollie panted, "and I'm going to beat you so many colors they'll wave you at the head of a gay pride parade."

"Why Ollie," Jack said, pulling himself to his feet on the coat rack. "I'd never guess you had the stones to get physical. I learn new things every fucking day, don't I?" This was far from ideal. If Heath was using violence, he thought Jack had done something that warranted violence. Heath wasn't a vicious cop, and Jack was covered in blood. A little worry, real and cold, stole in and curled itself in the bottom of Jack's stomach. Heath didn't like him and Heath didn't trust him, and the reverse was true with Jack. But Ollie had a badge, and Jack had a bloody knife and a raging hangover.

This time, Heath won.

Ollie kicked the door shut and faced Jack, his fists curling and uncurling as if his whole body was on a wire. "Where were you between one and four this morning?"

Jack slumped on the sofa, wiggling his jaw and hearing it click from where Ollie had belted him. "Here, I guess. Woke up here, at any rate."

"So you don't have an alibi," Ollie said. He'd gotten quiet, the anger bleeding into something more calculating.

"No," Jack sighed, rubbing his sore head. "But you knew that, Heath."

Jack recognized a fit-up when he saw one. The blood, the disappeared memory, and Heath at his door thinking he'd done wicked deeds needing punishment. It was on Jack to figure out exactly what brand of wickedness he was supposed to have done.

"I suppose I did," Ollie said. "So why don't you return the favor and tell me how you knew Damien Toskovitch? And while you're at it, Tommy Nelson and Robert Willis?"

"Who?" Jack said politely, patting himself down for a cigarette. He feigned interest while Ollie turned pink.

"Toskovitch is the Russian gent you stabbed six times this morning, Winter. Nelson and Willis are the two blokes kilt the same way as Fiona Hannigan, back at the start of your little adventure. Jesus, are you really that coldblooded?"

"Look," Jack said, exhaling. "I was at a club last night called Memento Mori, chasing a lead *you* blokes should have been onto weeks ago. I woke up here not twenty minutes ago after what you might call a bad end to a bad evening with no memory and a lump on my head the size of Victoria's crown jewels, and that's the truth, honest as whatever gods you believe in. I never heard of any Russians, and blokes, or anything else." He flicked ash off the end of his cigarette, that landed on Ollie's shoe like dirty London snow.

Ollie bent down with a smile that Jack could only describe as both wholly grim and entirely self-satisfied, and retrieved the key from the floor. "Oh really. What's this, then?"

Jack twitched. Stealing evidence didn't really help his protestations of innocence. And he *was* innocent, he was pretty sure. It took a lot more than drugs or hypnosis or a crack on the head to make a psychic do as you said against their will. Psychic talent was the lead-lined room of brains…hell to live in, but equally hard to see into.

"You tell me," he said to Heath. "Seems you've got me fitted for this, right and proper."

"This is Fiona Hannigan's key," Ollie said. "Don't play dumber than you look, Winter. It's embarrassing for us both."

"Sure you're not just embarrassed because I lifted it from you?" Jack asked, lacing his fingers behind his head. "Can't look very good to your powers that be, the DI who runs about hiring strange metaphysical consultants and then loses a piece of evidence. Sure you're not just taking out the old job stress on me, Ollie?"

Jack was prepared for yelling, storming about, more threats about the dead Russian and Heath's other cases from the same killer, whoever they were. The names were vaguely familiar, but he wasn't really in shape to stroll through his extensive index of tossers he'd used to know.

He wasn't prepared, however, for Ollie to crack him across the face again. Jack's cheek mushed against his teeth, and he tasted his own blood on his tongue. "Fuck me, Heath!" he shouted. "I know you're trying to frame me up but is that fucking necessary?"

"I've never framed one villain in my career," Ollie spit. "Not one, and I'll be fucked twice by a lightpost if I start with a waste of oxygen like you, Winter." He brandished the key, spotted with dried blood in Jack's fingerprint, in front of Jack's face. "*My* key is safe in evidence. That means *your* key came from before she was killed. Means you could have gone to her place any time you like, and you did, because you *knew* her and you *killed* her and you let me take you back there to get your jollies, you sick fucking piece of shit."

Jack's blood, which had been heating steadily in the face of Heath's yelling, cooled abruptly. "No. I took that key from you. Look again."

"Don't need to look, do I?" Heath said. "Went to her flat before I came here. Used my key. Wanted to check one more time, knowing the kind of bastard you are, see if you'd fingered any of her stuff we could use for forensic evidence to put you in Pentonville for a good long while."

Jack shook his head. He was numb, a curious buzzing in his hands, a roaring in his ears. "I didn't kill Fiona. I would never... I felt *sorry* for Fiona."

"Bet you did," Ollie agreed. A jangle, a flash of steel, and his handcuffs were off his belt and at the ready. "Bet if we ask the medical examiner to look again we'll find your DNA, showing us just how sorry you felt for her."

Ollie leaned down, to Jack's level, and the satisfaction on his face was practically pornographic. "I knew you was a bad penny, Winter. From the moment I clapped eyes on you. And now everyone will know what I do."

He straightened up, and gestured Jack with him. "Get up."

"This is a mistake..." Jack started, because now it really was. He could have worked out why he was supposed to have topped a mysterious Russian, but two blokes plus Fiona? Delicate, stupid, pretty Fiona? This was much more than a warning from Waverly to back off.

This was someone who truly wanted him rotting in a moldy cell, with only an amorous skinhead named Peaches for company.

Jack couldn't think of anyone who hated him that much.

But if he let Heath take him in, he'd never find out. Juries loved to hang junkies, even clean ones, for past offenses real or imaginary. Ollie would be a very credible witness. And Pete...what the fuck would happen to her? Her reputation would be shredded. She'd never work in law enforcement again. Every case she'd ever worked with the Met could come into question. Pete would lose even more than he would.

"Get. Up!" Ollie bellowed. He drew out his pistol. "I'm not a violent man, Winter, but frankly I'd love the excuse."

Jack stood, the strange tingle ebbing and flowing from his heart into his arms, his brain and everywhere. He recognized the sensation as shocked. He couldn't remember the last time he'd be shocked. It had literally been a decade or more.

"Heath," he tried one more time. "Don't do this. You don't understand, mate..."

Ollie holstered his pistol and unlocked his cuffs. "You're under the arrest for the murders of Fiona Hannigan and Damien Toskovitch. Anything you say may be taken down and may be used in evidence against you."

Jack held up his hands, and Ollie's free hand jumped back to his gun. "Don't make me do it, Winter."

The decision wasn't that hard, once Jack realized that he wasn't getting out of this by convincing Heath he hadn't gone on a mad slashing spree throughout the city. He dropped his hands. "Listen, Heath. I don't expect you to believe me..."

"Good," Heath snapped. "Because I'm through listening to what spews out of that shit-hole you call a mouth, Winter."

In reply, Jack snapped his fist forward, hitting Ollie in the nose. He felt the cartilage crunch under his hand and Ollie let out a roar of pain.

With Heath off balance, Jack pulled a bit of power into the forefront of his brain, feeling the fizz and crackle of the Black as it rushed to fill the void he'd opened.

Jack threw the freezing curse on Heath with a word. "*Sciotha.*"

Ollie went rigid and started to choke as he fell backwards onto the carpet, thrashing his head back and forth like an upended turtle. Blood was still dribbling from his nose at a fair clip.

Leaning down, Jack felt for Heath's wallet. "It'll wear off in an hour or two if I'm not around to keep it on," he told Heath. "It's just paralysis, nothing fancy or frightening. So stop thrashing before all that blood runs back into your throat and chokes you to death, and you'll be all right." Jack took thirty pounds from Heath's wallet, the DI's handcuffs, and his stun gun. Toting a firearm around would just get him pinched again, and he was rubbish with them anyway.

"You're fucking dead," Heath croaked, pain and magic muting his voice. "You hear me, Winter? I clap eyes on you again, I'm fitting you for a box."

Jack nodded. "Fair enough." He shoved his prizes into his pockets, grabbed his leather, pulling it on over his bare, bloody torso, and headed out the door.

twelve

AVOIDING Ollie's mates in uniform was easy enough, and Jack slipped into the Whitechapel tube station without any further need to smack anyone in the gob. His fist smarted. He didn't like fighting up close if he could help it. Used to, when he was twenty-two and dumb, but nowadays he was too old and something always got skinned or broken or dislocated when he actually had to resort to hitting some cunt to knock him down.

He took an inbound train for the City, and wished like fuck he'd gotten a mobile like Pete was always nagging him about. Then again, it was probably good he hadn't—bad enough that the Met could find him on any of the thousands of CCTV cameras trained on central London, he didn't need bloody satellites from space honing in on his GPS signal. Plus, mobiles tended to die horrible deaths around Jack, more from neglect than from any field his talent exuded. He'd dunked them in loos, lost them under the wheels of a minicab, and gotten one lifted by an exotic dancer in Leeds, although to be fair he considered that one more of a trade.

St. Pancras was a crush, as usual, and Jack disembarked with a horde of tourists, keeping his head low and his face shielded. Ollie wouldn't be free for a few hours yet, but if he decided to use London's very own Big Brother network to track Jack's movements, Jack would just as soon he didn't give Heath an easy time.

He exited the station by the taxi entrance, walking past St. Pancras Church toward Russell Square. While he walked, letting himself blend in with the madness of taxis, buses, tourists and harried locals at this, one of the centers of the city, he tried to breathe and to figure out what the fuck had just happened.

First order of business was to find Pete and get her to find out exactly what Heath had on him. Then he could figure out who was trying to fuck him, find the bastard, and show him by hard, repeated kicks to the groin exactly how wrong of an idea it was.

Jack ducked into to a phone booth, keeping a mindful eye on the two uniformed Met officers standing at the corner of the Square, across from the Victorian facade of the Hotel Russell. He needed to get a shirt, and wash the blood off.

First things first.

He dropped his coins and dialed Pete's mobile. She picked up on the first ring, already going at a shout. "Jack? What the *fuck* is going on? Where are you?"

Jack held the phone away from his ear. "How'd you know it was me, luv?"

"Who else would it be?" she sighed. "Jack, why does the Met think you killed Fiona?"

"It wasn't me," he said. "Pete, somebody's fitting me for a frame-up and I'd really like to know why."

Silence. Jack listened to the traffic for three heartbeats. "Pete?"

"I know," she sighed. "I know you, Jack. This isn't you."

He drummed his fingers on top of the phone box. "So what do we do?"

"Did you hurt Ollie?" Pete asked. Jack blew out his breath. "He'll live."

"Jack, for the love of sweet baby Christ. How could you assault an officer with the shite you're already in?" Pete sighed heavily into the phone.

"He did have it coming," Jack protested.

"Jack!"

"All right, all right," he said. "Listen, I'm supposed to have killed a bloke named Damien Toskovitch sometime last night. Same way as Fiona and the other two wossnames, which Heath apparently was holding back for a birthday surprise."

"The Met's got a bulletin on you, I can tell you that much right now," Pete said. "Stay low."

"Already doing that, aren't I?" Jack said. "Remember, luv— I've had a lot more experience dodging the plods than you."

"And gaining more by the second," Pete said. "They'll have a trace on my line as soon as Ollie gets himself together. I'm going to dump my phone. Where should I meet you?"

The uniforms walked off, one speaking into his radio. Jack felt his chest relax a centimeter. "Brompton Cemetery," he said. "Soon as you can."

"All right," Pete agreed. "Give me a couple of hours to work my magic with my friends in IT at the Met, and I'll be there.

And Jack?" Her voice pitched up, and Jack allowed himself the small comfort of imagining Pete was worried about him.

"Yeah, luv?"

"Watch your arse," Pete said, and hung up.

Jack stepped out of the booth and hailed a cab. It was a bit of a trial to convince the driver he wanted to take a shirtless and mussed aging punk to Peckham, even in broad daylight, but Ollie's thirty pounds up front talked the bloke into it.

The zombie guarding Gemma's flat was considerably less lively, and Jack wrinkled his nose at the pungency that clung to the thing's flesh like a cheap polyester shirt. "You ought to liven him up," he told Gemma when she came down. "Give him some camphor and incense like the Egyptians did it. Have a necromancer in to paint him up in some reviving symbols." He fanned away the stench of decomposition. "At least stick one of those little cardboard Christmas trees 'round his neck."

Gemma looked Jack over. "Your blood, or another bloke's?"

Jack rolled his eyes. "Please. Even I'm not mean enough to survive a cut like that."

Gemma's mouth twitched. "I suppose not. Come upstairs."

Instead of breaking out the whiskey and the barbed conversation, Gemma led Jack into an en suite roughly the size of his bedroom, and started a stream of water into a pristine, cubist bathtub. She gestured at Jack. "Get all that off."

He left the encrusted denim gladly, his boots and leather less quickly. "Don't you dare throw those away," he told Gemma. He wasn't worried about being naked in front of her—he didn't have anything to be shy about and she'd seen him in a far worse state.

"Your jaw is puffy," Gemma said. She added oil from a small green bottle to the bathwater and then gesture at Jack. "Get in. I'll bring you ice."

"You're being awfully civil to me, Gem," Jack said. "Didn't think I was your type." He sank gingerly into the water. It was scalding hot, scented of something sweet and sultry that Jack recalled but couldn't place, and lifted the outermost layer of the blood off him. The blood and the oil stained the water golden-pink.

Gemma came back with a cup of tea, no additives, and placed it on the rim of the tub. "Christ," she said. "You look like some kind of gladiator."

Jack gave her a lazy smile. He was still fucking rattled and had no idea what the fuck was going on, but Gemma was still very attractive and he was still very naked. "That make you my winnings, then?"

Gemma gave him one of her rare, genuine smiles. "You play your cards right, Jack, I might make an exception for you. 'Course, I'd like you better if you had a lovely pair of tits to go with that pretty blond head."

Jack laughed. "I don't think I've ever heard you talk that way, Gem."

She patted him on the shoulder, her hand lingering on his tattoo ink. He had a lot of them. *Always have more ink than scars* was the advice his first teacher, Seth McBride, had given him, and while most of what Seth said was utter shit, that bit was sound.

"There's a lot you don't know, Jack," Gemma said, and her translucent glass-bead eyes went distant. In that moment, Gemma wasn't hollow. But she wasn't full of anything good, either.

Then she chased it away, and she was the poker-faced pusher he'd come to know and love. "Drink up. I've got you clean clothes, and my driver can take you wherever you need to go. I imagine Miss Bleeding Heart is rather worried about you."

"She's not," Jack said. "Trust me. But I do need to get out of here and figure out who's fitting me for four murders, sadly."

"Of course." Gemma stood. "Drink your tea," she admonished, when Jack sank deeper into the water and groaned.

"No offense, luv," he said, his voice coming out slow, "but drinking drinks is exactly what got me into this mess." He could stay in this water forever. Stay with Gemma forever. Gemma, at least, never judged him. And if she didn't like boys, well. He could get to like watching.

Jack thrashed upright as the water reached his chin. Where the fuck was this coming from? He admitted he thought with his cock as much as the next man, but he was looking at potentially being locked away in the sort of prison where magic did no good whatsoever if he didn't sort this out, and he was getting horny instead?

"It's all right," Gemma said. The sound of her voice was very high and far off, as if Jack were down a deep tunnel.

"It…it is?" he managed. He just wanted to fall back, to hold his breath and sink down…

"Yes," Gemma said, and he felt her cool long-fingered hand on his forehead, smoothing his hair back. "The tea isn't drugged," Gemma whispered. "It's the bathwater."

Jack looked up into her eyes. They were full again, her light brows drawn into a dark furrow. She sighed. "I'm sorry, Jack. Really bloody sorry."

"Oh fuck," Jack said, and slid under for the second time in as many days.

His last thought before blackness was this was a sorry fucking habit to have picked up.

thirteen

HE was dreaming again. Jack knew it was a dream because his arms were free of both ink and track marks, and the scars that he'd given himself in a cheap Dublin hotel room were fresh and pink once more.

Fiona stood in front of him, leather skirt slipping down her hips. Her fishnets were shredded at the knees from going down on a concrete floor and her cut-down Siouxsie jersey sliding off her shoulders. Pete had that same shirt. It was so old it was coming apart, and she kept it together with safety pins and prayers.

"It hurt," Fiona said. "In case you were wondering, Jack. It hurt like knives."

"Fuck off," Jack mumbled, or tried to mumble. "Your own fault, wasn't it?"

"You blame me for wanting something better?" Fiona said. "After I got too old and fat for Chester, you think it was easy being a girl with no brains and no prospects? I learned how to bind ghosts, and I did it, because otherwise I'd be nothing."

"You always had brains," Jack said. "You just didn't use them, luv." In the dream, he was clean from blood. Only the echo of his own voice, the slow bell tone of heavy-duty sedatives, gave a clue that he wasn't awake. "Preferred to have gullible blokes around to pull your fat out of the fire. Easier, I'd imagine."

"Not this time," Fiona sighed. "Prince Charming put a sword in my back. He showed me…he showed me so many things, but he was just filling me up, like all the others. With his own ideas and his own magic. I'm alone, Jack…alone as I ever was…"

"Christ," Jack sighed. "I'd really love to wake up now, please."

"Fine," Fiona snarled, and just for a moment he saw something rise up behind her, the black spirit that she'd bound to her body. It had eyes and a face, a body that was just a black mass. The eyes glared at Jack, and he felt his skin begin to burn. When he looked down he was in flames, the blue fire of his own magic eating him alive, and then he turned to ash, inch by inch, until he woke up screaming.

"Good bloody lord!" Gemma shouted. "I've been trying to wake you up for the last hour!" She exhaled, slumping back against the wall. "Thought I gave you too much dream-time."

Jack took quick inventory. It was different from the hangover variety—check that you're still alive. His head pounded and he was chained to a dripping pipe a meter above his head, very tightly and efficiently, with some rusty old-fashioned prison shackles.

Right. See where the fuck you are and what the bastards have done to you. It was a basement, some kind of industrial space with warnings spray painted on the brick. The floor was dirt, packed hard and the lower down the wall Jack's eye went, the older the brick got.

Huge bloody help. They could be anywhere under central London. Most of the buildings there had grown up on the ruins of the Great Fire in 1666, and their cellars all looked the same.

He appeared to be intact, aside from the raging headache and the fact that he was wearing a pair of silk pyjama bottoms. And, of course, chained to a fucking pipe in a fucking cellar.

The only consolation was that Gemma appeared to be in much the same situation. She flexed her hands uselessly against her own cuffs and then hissed. "Fuck me, this is not my day."

A small line of red worked its way down her blond temple as she struggled, and Jack tilted his head at her. "So what'd I miss, Gem?"

"That bastard," she spat. "That ruddy bastard, he *told* me if I turned you over he'd quit coming around my patch, trying to cut into things."

"Didn't work out?" Jack guessed.

Gemma let loose with another string of invective, both far more creative and far more varied than he'd give a West End girl like her credit for. "I'm here, aren't I?" she said finally. "Turns out he only wanted you. He had no interest in my patch. Set me out on a fucking fishing line and I walked right into it. Christ."

Jack leaned his head against the brick. Far off, he could hear a rush, the echoing bleats of horns. But he wasn't going anywhere, not until the cobwebs cleared out of his head enough to slip the locks. "What'd you give me, Gemma?" he said. "It's important, if we want to get out of here."

"It's a Fae nectar," she said. "Sends you off to dreamland, makes all your fondest wishes come true. It's why you wanted to fuck me brainless right before you went under. Side effect. I have a good street trade going on that stuff, actually."

"Yeah, well, it doesn't work so nicely on psychics," Jack told her. "Sales tip." Fiona's bony little body, her hands with their shredded nails clawing for him, reached out from his sight for a moment before the drugs washed it away again.

"It'll wear off in a few hours," Gemma said.

Jack listened to doors open and close, bootfalls on the floor above. Something familiar, thin and twitchy and magic, filtered down through his layers of stupefaction, but it was gone again before he could grab for it. Still, it meant whoever had crossed Gemma was upstairs, and soon they'd be down here, doing fuck knew what to the pair of them.

"I don't think we have a few hours," he told Gemma.

"No," she sighed. "Suppose not. Always thought it would be in my flat. Something nice and dignified, from a nice dignified man in a suit. Two in the back of the head. Small caliber, so my dad could have a proper funeral." She swallowed hard, but her hollowness was tears now, and one squeezed down her cheek. "Oh Christ, my dad...he won't know what's happened if I don't call."

Jack rattled his shackles, testing the weight. The chain was rusty, but the iron was solid, and it wasn't doing any favors for his talent. "Gemma," he said. "I need you to keep your head on."

"You probably think it's funny," she said. "Your queer ice queen pusher having a dad. I do, Jack. We speak every Sunday."

"I don't think it's amusing in the least," Jack said. "In fact, this is the least amusing situation involving lesbians, handcuffs and illegal drugs I've ever found meself in." He caught

Gemma's eye. "But I know you, woman, and you've got ice cold venom for blood, so help me, yeah? I'm not used to this gangster shite."

Gemma nodded, bit down hard on her lip, and when she looked up she was the hard, hollow bitch on wheels he recognized.

The heavy boots descended the stairs, and someone fiddled with an ancient, finicky lock on the other side of the basement door.

"By the way," Jack whispered. "Why am I in these poncey lounging pants?"

"I dressed you," Gemma murmured. "Didn't seem right sending you to your doom stark bloody naked, though I'm sure that's how you'd prefer it."

"Cheers," Jack said, and didn't get out any more before the door swung open.

The bouncer from Memento Mori, made exponentially huger by a shiny satin windcheater and enormous boots, ducked his head to enter the cellar.

"Oh, good," Jack said. "The stand-up comedian has arrived."

The bouncer knocked his head against the pipes and let out an actual snarl. Jack tsked. "You have *got* to tell us what they're feeding you, mate. You're the Incredible Chav Hulk."

Closing the space between them, the bouncer backhanded Jack across the face. His head took a chip out of the bricks, and Jack felt a pair of his molars loosen. Blood filled up his mouth.

"I fucking *hate* Jonathan Ross, you cunt," the bouncer growled.

Jack spat blood on his boot. "Well," he agreed, "he's not everyone's cup of tea."

He didn't bother asking why they were here, in a basement, why the chains and why the fit-up. Whoever had put him here knew that if he was in a tight spot he'd run to Gemma. Leverage Gemma, leverage Jack, and put the Met off their scent in the process.

If Jack thought about it, it was a good plan, a wicked, knife-like plan. One worthy of him, in the bad old days.

The bouncer went to an old workbench and picked up a glass jar and a paintbrush. "You going to make trouble?" he asked, with a hopeful lilt to his voice.

"Mate, I'm hung over and chained to a fucking pipe," Jack sighed. "What do you think?"

"Just hold still," the bouncer muttered, and dipped his brush into the jar. The rank, coppery scent of animal blood hit Jack's nose.

"Fuck off," he said. "You're not putting that on me."

"Like you said," the bouncer put the tip of the brush against Jack's chest, "you can't do nothing, can you?"

Gemma watched him, perfectly still, and Jack looked to her, then around the small, low space again.

Nothing good ever came of covering yourself in blood. A drop or two here and there to shut a circle or seal up a hex nice and tight, that was par for the course. But slopping animal blood all over a bloke—that never ended in anything but tears and/or decapitation.

"I could've taken your girl's head off," said the bouncer as he worked. "But I didn't. Our mutual friend said leave her alive, for old time's sake."

"How magnanimous of you," Gemma murmured.

The bouncer stepped back and looked at his work. "That'll do. Now you just hang there like a good man, and wait."

He put down the blood and the brush and left, and Jack tried to see what was on his chest. It crawled, whatever it was, with black magic and the same oily power as the binding hex that he'd found in Fiona's things.

"It's nothing good," Gemma told him. "I don't know much about markings and sigils and that stuff, but it's making my head hurt."

That cemented Jack's decision. "We're getting out of here," he said. "Before Mr. Old Times comes back. Got any angry exes up your sleeve, Gem?"

"None with a male pronoun attached," Gemma said. She flexed her hands, only once. Jack tried the locks again, and got a little movement this time. Whatever was in the blood, be it silver nitrate or the ashes of a sacred bone or the plain old herbs and spices hippie sorcerers loved to muck about with was at least chasing away the hangover.

"I think there's a door over there," Gemma said. Jack's skin was starting to prickle and burn, and he could feel the blood dribbling over his ribcage and into the hollow of his hip bones. Whatever his unseen new friend was calling to him with the blood, it was what had gotten loose from Gemma, and it didn't feel any less angry.

Jack shut his eyes, tight and tried for the locks again. One gave, just a bit, and then popped open. The other soon followed. His head was beginning to throb, the bright, dreamy slippage of a fever washing over him.

Gemma's shackles were a bit easier, even if the room was beginning to wash out around him, the colors bleeding as the Black fought to boil up and drown him in a well of his sight.

Her hand was icy cold on his skin, and Jack could hear whispering and faint screaming, knew that the thing that had killed Fiona was almost upon him.

And then, they were out of the stifling cellar and there was a hot, sour, sooty wind on his face, pushing dirt and dust down his throat.

Far off, Jack heard the rumble and shriek of a tube train, and Gemma pulled him along, until they came to an access hatch with stern warnings about use by London Underground employees only.

"I should be disappeared," Gemma said. "He knows where I live. I have to clear out of town."

Jack nodded. The heat and the tightness eased a bit, but he still felt as if he were going to drop like a stone on the floor of the access tunnel. "You going to be all right, Gem?"

"Sure," she said. "I'll go to my dad's. He lives out in the Midlands nowadays. Local town for local people, all that shit. He'll be glad to see me." She turned his face from side to side. "You going to send someone after me to do in my kneecaps?"

Jack leaned against the wall and tried to wipe some of the sweat from his face. "Fuck no, Gem. Just go. You've done enough."

She bit her lip for a moment, but the she opened the door and stepped on onto the platform, noise and people and light sweeping her away.

fourteen

NIGHTFALL was long gone, encroaching into middle age, by the time Jack cleaned up, nicked some real clothes and reached the gates of Brompton Cemetery. They were locked, of course, the high Victorian arch that signaled the entrance barred with iron gates bubbled in rust.

Jack convinced the locks open. It felt like someone had thrust a butter knife inside his skull and scraped out the last contents to put on toast. The drugs and the magic and the rest of it were still battering his body.

He needed sleep. Sleep, fags, a shag and a drink.

Heroin.

No. Jack snarled at his own treacherous gray matter. Whatever he needed, smack was not going to help him get it.

Brompton Cemetery, the largest of the Victorian cemeteries in London, was a massive place, chock full of the dead. A wide avenue ran down the center, dividing the land in two, and at the end a great pavilion and chapel waited, domed roof and open-air columns making the place seem like something older, darker than twenty-first century England. The place was a great sprawling monument to the dead, and they clustered here thicker than grass, a thorny thicket of ghosts and spirit shreds just waiting for him to open his eyes.

Jack listened to his own bootfalls on the cracked asphalt as he passed angels and demons, white as phantoms in the moonlight and the glow from the city all around. The limestone monuments had black hollows for eyes, and they followed him in the dark. Jack walked until one of the shadows moved.

"Where the *fuck*," Pete said, "have you been?"

Jack rolled his neck. His wrists were still burning from the iron manacles, and he hurt everywhere. "It's been a long day, luv. Put it that way."

Pete closed the distance between them and wrapped her arms around his torso, hard. She put her cheek on his chest and went silent for the space of a few heartbeats. She was strong, for her size, and Jack let himself lean against her for a moment. He stayed quiet, as well.

"I was worried," Pete said at last, her voice muffled by his clothes. "I thought…" She pulled back and fingered the silk jacket and the cheap souvenir shirt under it. "Where the fuck are your clothes?"

"Good question," he said. "Better question: how am I supposed to have topped Damien Whosit?"

"Toskovitch," Pete said. She pulled out a disposable mobile, the kind you could pick up for ten quid in any electronics shop. "I had a friend in Comms who owes me a favor, but I couldn't get much—just an address and a cause of death." She showed

Jack the screen. "He lives out in Chiswick. And his throat was slashed, just like Fiona and the other two."

"Chiswick?" Jack fidgeted against the cold inside his jacket. "Christ, if I lived there I'd slice me own jugular."

"They found your fingerprints," Pete said, her voice barely rising over the traffic and the noise of the wind between the tombs. "It doesn't look very good, Jack."

"Pete, any sod could have lifted my prints from anywhere I've been in the last two weeks," Jack sighed. "I'm a bit handsy, in case you hadn't noticed."

"Oh, I've noticed, believe it," Pete said, giving him a significant crook of her eyebrows. She lit a cigarette and exhaled. "I'm quite mad at Ollie, you know. A serial killer running about London and he didn't breathe a word."

"Probably wants that promotion you'd get, you were still on the job," Jack said. "That, and he thinks you're too good for me."

"I am too good for you," Pete said, but not meanly. "'Least you're not a serial killer. Curse of four, my Da used to say."

Jack accepted the fag she handed him, lit it, and smoked. It didn't do much for his racing heart, but it made his hands stopp shaking. "Your old man had a saying for everything."

"You know why it's the curse of four," Pete sucked on her cigarette and exhaled a smoke dragon. "Not three or five but four? Three, your bloke is still learning his trade. Still getting comfortable with the idea of taking a life, of getting off to his particular brand of kink. Four..." Pete flicked the end of her fag into the weeds. "Four is when he gets really good."

Jack ground out his own under his boot. "Lucky me."

Pete nodded. "And the question remains."

"Two questions," Jack supplied.

"Who's fitting you for these deaths..." Pete started.

"And who's binding ghosts in London?" Jack finished.

Pete tilted the information about Toskovitch toward him. "Well, we've got a fresh crime scene—what say we go have a look?"

fifteen

TOSKOVITCH'S semi-detached house was a far cry from Fiona's dour flat. There were neat flower boxes under the windows and a welcome mat. The door was sealed with police tape and Pete pointed out an unmarked black sedan at the corner. "Coppers," she said. "Keep walking and we'll swing through the gardens on the next block."

"Won't they be watching the back door?" Jack murmured. Pete snorted under her breath.

"Trust me, the Met doesn't have the inclination or the manpower to be that thorough."

After an interminable climb over garden walls and a yapping-at by several small and unpleasant mop-shaped dogs, Jack landed in the soft earth beneath Damien Toskovitch's kitchen window.

Pete went to work on the door, and he let her. It'd be better not to add breaking and entering to the list of what Heath thought he'd done, even via his talent.

Inside, the house was as obsessively neat as the garden. To Jack's naked eye, Damien Toskovitch was about as magical as his electric kettle. But the signs were there—the orderly glass apothecary jars filled with herbs and twisted, mummified frogs. A violin hung on a stand in the front room along with dog-eared sheet music, and an ancient television was nearly obscured by a stack of handwritten grimoires in Russian.

"'M going upstairs," Jack said to Pete.

"I'll keep an eye," she said quietly.

Toskovitch's bedroom was a study in prissiness—the bed was made with military corners and a sad football flag from the Russian national club drooped above it, the only sign of a personality. Jack went through the drawers, found a solitary porno mag, a copy of a cheap thriller and some aspirin, and was contemplating kicking over the mattress when the hairs on the back of his neck lifted straight up, like tiny television aerials.

Blackness curled at the edges of his vision, and his second eye, his sight, sparked and irised like the lens of a camera.

Something was in the room, just over his shoulder, floating in the corner.

It's all a bit grim, isn't it? said a voice cut from cooled marble and honed with a bronze knife. *Chiswick. In my day, such a place would have been burned.*

Jack tried to move, but it was Fiona's flat all over again—the sensation of being filled up with something not himself, the smothering of a dead thing sharing his flesh, his own being pressed into a corner of his brain that was too tight and too close. The spot where he'd washed the blood from his chest began to burn again.

"You stick around to jump into a new body, then?" he asked. "Looks like it's just me and a few fat policemen. Choice cuts of sorcerer are a bit thin on the ground."

Mage, I do not need a body, the voice snarled. *I am older than that. Older than legend. Wickeder than flesh.*

"Oh, crack on," Jack sighed. "What do you want from me?"

To go somewhere more conducive to conversation, for a start, the ghost purred. Jack felt a shadow pass across his mind, and then the world tilted sideways and he fell.

In the next blink of an eye, he stood in a library. Carpet muffled his boots, and books crammed the shelves floor to ceiling.

A man in a wing back chair—not a body, just a suggestion of a man—stared up at Jack. *That's more like it.*

Jack looked up at the ceiling, where old-fashioned electric bulbs spat and buzzed, and all around. The room had no windows. "Where the fuck are we?"

Still in that disreputable bedroom, have no fear, said the ghost. *I just prefer not to look at the detritus of that bastard's meaningless life.*

The low, reddish light didn't make putting a face to the ghost easy, but Jack tried. Round cheeks, a high forehead, eyes older than standing stones burning out of a childish face. The ghost lifted its thin upper lip in a sneer. *"Like what you see, boyo?"*

Jack lifted his finger, tried to ignore the sick, twisting feeling being so close to the thing sent over his whole body, like seasickness on dry land. "I know you."

The ghost smiled, and inclined his head. *And I of you, crowmage. I hear through the wires and witchling byways that you've taken to using my moniker.* The smile got wider. *Wickedest in the world.*

"Oh, hell," Jack said. "You're Aleister fucking Crowley."

Pleased to meet you, said the ghost. *At least I believe I am. I've been with that tiresome sod Toskovitch for a very long time.*

The severe black suit, the high forehead, the changeable fire in the eyes—Jack had seen it glaring back at him from at least a hundred pictures. "You…" he said. "Did you kill Fiona, Crowley?"

My boy, Crowley said, and his outline shimmered a bit. If ghosts could have laughed, Crowley would be grinning. *I didn't even kill Toskovitch. That was a very bad dog, a bad boy who's been let far too much chain.*

"I…well…" Jack didn't often find himself at a loss for words. He wasn't sure he liked it very much. "How did you…come to be here?"

Toskovitch bound me, Crowley said. *And another before him. He was fat, old, but not stupid. He dropped dead and Toskovitch took over.*

"So let me see if I understand." Jack's throat itched and he wished for a fag. "You were bound…voluntarily?"

Of course not, Crowley snarled. *My intent was to never die in the first place. When a mage such as myself dies, we leave a certain…residue. A residue that a skilled ghost-binder can graft to their own soul. Keeping us close. Feeding us just enough life to keep us from crossing through the Bleak Gates. Like a battery, dear boy.*

"Pardon me," Jack said. "And no disrespect to your whole hippie commune-sex magic-demon shagging bit—but *why* would a living human being want to tether himself to a poxy ghost for all eternity?"

the curse of FOUR

Well, Crowley's eyebrow arched, *certainly not for the conversation.* He sighed, and shimmered upright, spreading his arms. *Why does any mage, anyone in the Black do anything, my dear? Power. He fed the ghost and I fed him. Toskovitch. He could do things beyond human ability, as long as I was at his side.*

Crowley sighed, and twitched his cuffs. *Pedestrian things, really. The others…they made better use of their spirits. Most especially, your friend Fiona.*

"Why?" Jack bored into Crowley with his eyes, a contest he frankly wasn't sure he'd win. Crowley had one of the sharpest drill-bit gazes he'd ever encountered. "Who did she have as her…battery?"

Possibly the only man in the world more terrifying than myself, Crowley purred.

Jack snorted. "Right. I'd be pissing meself in terror at the sight of that forehead of yours, that's for sure."

Crowley snarled, and flickered in and out, coming to rest with his hand on Jack's face. The cold went through Jack's bones, and his sight screamed. He could see Crowley as he truly was, not as the man's illusion showed him. His eyes were black, screaming pits, and his flesh was rotting away from his fire-blackened bones as the rot and corruption of Crowley's demon-fueled magic swirled around them. *You dare,* Crowley hissed. *You're not so wicked as you imagine, crow-mage. Not by half.*

Behind Crowley, Jack saw a great black whirlwind open up, a hole all the way down to the Bleak Gates.

Not the Bleak Gates. The Underworld was a foreign place, a place no living man was meant to tread, but Jack had been to its doorstep before. This was something different. There was something hungry and dripping with malice beyond the screaming void, and Jack saw long black fingers of magic reaching for them, like ink spilled into clear water. Blood feathering out to feed the sharks.

"Crowley!" Jack said. "What the fuck is going on?"

A new binding, the ghost sighed. *A new master, a new parasite. Goodbye, crow-mage.*

"Wait!" Jack shouted. The roar of the Black rose beyond hearing, until it was just a dull throbbing in his skull, vibrating in his back teeth. "Crowley, who's doing this? Who's binding you?"

A far worse specimen of the human race than either of us, Crowley sighed. *Even worse than his mad dog, the deathless monk.*

"Fuck," Jack snarled, trying to hold on to the ghost. It was, he realized, utterly fruitless.

He hates you more than anyone on earth, Crowley hissed. *How long of a list can that be?*

The binding grabbed hold of him. And with a memory of a scream, Crowley disappeared.

"Jack."

Jack was on his back, on Toskovitch's lumpy rug. Pete knelt beside him, shining her penlight into his pupils. Jack screwed his face up. "Ow."

"You were ranting and raving," Pete said shortly. "We need to move before the Met busts in here. They're slow but they will eventually respond to a grown man screaming his head off in the blessed suburbs."

"All right, all right," Jack grumbled as she yanked him to his feet. Getting too close to spirits always gave him a hangover. His stomach lurched, and he stumbled as Pete pulled him through the back door and out into the gardens.

The cool air took a bit of the edge off, and he managed to scale the wall behind Pete and drop into the parking avenue behind the row of houses.

"All right, what now?" Pete said as they walked, skirting the corner where the Met officers were parked. "All that yelling better have been worth something."

"Yeah, perhaps," Jack said absently. He fingered the key he'd stolen from Heath. "I have something I need to check up on. Something in this bloody Chinese puzzle box is a missing piece and I need it."

Pete stopped under a streetlight and put her hand on his chin, turning his face this way and that. Her touch prickled his skin, and Jack leaned into it, pressing his cheek into her hand.

"You're not going to be fucking stupid about this, are you?" Pete said. "I can't hold off Ollie forever."

"I'll try," Jack said. "Pete…"

She dropped the hand. "Forget it, Jack. I know it's useless telling you to be careful." She shrugged deeper into her jacket as the mist skirled around them, trapping them together under a bell jar of light.

"Still like to hear it," Jack murmured.

"But you won't be careful," Pete sighed. She rubbed her knuckles down his cheek, and then tucked her hand back into her pocket. "You're never careful."

Jack lifted his shoulders. "Worked out all right so far." He turned and stepped into the fog, feeling in his leather for a fag.

Pete's voice carried over his shoulder. "Until it doesn't."

SiXteen

FIONA'S flat had taken on the staleness of a mausoleum—
that pseudo-air that clings around closed places, and old places,
and death.

A crew from the crime scene division at the Met had carted
away the rug, and leftover chalk marks and pieces of marking
tape were everywhere. Fingerprinting powder cast an antique
pall over Fiona's furniture.

Jack sneezed.

He didn't turn on any lights—the streetlamp drifted in
through the sprigged curtains, and what furniture Fiona had
possessed was out of the way. In the kitchen, her catchall drawer
yielded chalk and a few stubby candles that smelled like chemical
oranges. It would be enough for what Jack had in mind.

He went back to the sitting room and knelt in the middle
of the floor. From memory instead of sight, he began to draw.

Calling a ghost, in the scheme of all magic, wasn't terribly
hard. It was even less so with the sight. Jack drew the symbols

by feel, by memory, and lit the candles with his lighter, placing them at the head and foot of the chalk marks.

That was all you had to do to make the dead appear. That, and a little bit of blood, and talent. Jack sliced his thumb open on the edge of his flick knife and squeezed what felt like four or five fat droplets onto the chalk.

The feeling he'd encountered when he first walked in with Heath returned, as if a slow tide were rising around his ankles.

Jack added one last step to the ritual. He took out the bit of nightsong orchid that Gemma had given him and put it on his tongue. The flower was milky and redolent with nectar, with a sharp bitter undertone like a poisoned sweet.

He bit down, and chewed until the venom in the petals coated his tongue. Nightsong, like most Fae plants, was a powerful psychotropic.

Jack had never been overly fond of tripping. He saw enough visions without chemical aids. Seeing the dead day in and day out quickly lost its charm.

But he had to see what Fiona had seen. The ghost who'd stood over her as she died.

He opened his eyes.

I know you, the ghost said, voice scraping across Jack's mind like razor wire. *You came before. With the policeman.*

Jack looked the man up and down. A full beard obscured his face and his body was a black smear, washing out to nothing a few inches short of the floor. The ghost was like an ink stain dissolving under rain water, except for his eyes, which burned with a life that put Crowley's slick, held-together specter to shame.

"I thought you'd be taller," he said at last.

the curse of FOUR

The man in the monk's robe smirked. *Likewise, crow-mage.*

He moved, and Jack found himself flat on his back, with Grigorii Rasputin's hands around his throat. The nightsong orchid opened up a vast well in his brain, and the cold, reptile part of him recognized the cold wind of the Underworld on his face. He was slipping, falling toward the ghost.

I will not be bound, Rasputin hissed. *I endured and at last, I am free.*

Jack shoved, with all of his power, reaching out for the cold, iron magic of the summoning circle. He squeezed his thumb in his fist hard, and felt a gush of warm blood. He was still alive.

"Then why," he wheezed at Rasputin, "are you still here?"

The ghost let him go abruptly, and Jack's head thumped against the floorboards. His vision bled away at the edges and he saw shreds of the gray sky that flew over the Underworld. The nightsong orchid created the twilight death—the illusion of dying, and let you brush the edges of the next world.

Jack just had to be careful he could come back.

You seem to know quite a lot, crow-mage, said Rasputin. *You tell me.*

"Fiona and Toskovitch and them," Jack rasped. He wanted to sit up, but he was drifting. "They find ghosts—strong ghosts, mage and sorcerer ghosts—and they bind them. Use them as batteries to juice up their own talents. Fucking stupid if you ask me."

Closer, said Rasputin. *But not the true picture. You only see what you wish to see.*

"Somebody's been murdering these sods—not that binding a ghost will net you an invitation to be knighted," Jack said. His throat burned where the ghost had touched him, hot and chill prickles like frostbite. "And now that someone has decided, for some reason, to fit me up for the killings and then…" He looked up at Rasputin, where the monk stood impassively staring straight ahead. "I ask again: why are you still here?"

He said he'd free me, Rasputin said. *After our bargain was done. And it is, now. Toskovitch was the last.*

"You killed them," Jack said. "He fiddled with Fiona's binding and sent you out to do the first two."

He'll keep his word, Rasputin whispered stonily.

"No," Jack sighed. "No, he won't." The orchid sat heavily on his tongue and in his throat, slowly depressing his breathing. Soon enough, he'd pass out, suffocate, and be dead for real.

You are a man of lies, crow-mage.

"And you're a man of being a great bloody arse, if you think you can trust some murderous bastard who'd try and free four of the worst spirits in existence." Jack's heartbeat was fading out of his ears. The skies were becoming darker, encroaching thunderheads over the spires of the great iron city where the dead resided.

He had to wrap this up.

"Just think about it," Jack told the ghost. "It took ten men to kill you the first time. You didn't stay around this long being a trusting soul, Grigorii. And neither did I."

His vision faded, the black vignette drawing down to a pinhole. "You help me, Rasputin," Jack murmured, hearing his words run together into a melody played on bone pipes, a record playing backwards. "And I'll help…I'll help you…"

Light burned out his vision, and the hands of the dead wrapped around his arms, rotting and encased in their shrouds.

Jack tried to fight, but the orchid's poison had reduced his nervous system to short circuits.

"Calm the fuck down, Winter, or I'll stun you," a voice commanded. "Oh, hell, who'm I kidding? You fucking tosser, after what you did I'm going to stun you anyway."

Electric fire danced up Jack's ribcage, straight into his heart, and abruptly the Underworld tore off his eyes and he could see the world of the living again. A uniformed Met officer was shining a torch into his eyes. He was on his knees, looking up into a smug, fat, familiar Yorkshire farmer face.

Jack said, "Fuck me," and threw up on Ollie Heath's shoes.

seventeen

THE fluorescent bulb above Jack's head buzzed, the slow dull buzzing that mirrored the ache in his skull.

Heath snapped his file folder open on the table, straightened his cuffs and tie. There was no evidence of a night spent on Jack's floor except in the blue half-moons under his eyes. "You'll pardon the wait," Ollie said. "I've been in the gents trying to wash your bloody upchuck off my favorite pair of brogues."

Jack put his forehead down on his arms. Ollie's handcuffs were too tight. His whole skin was too tight. His eyes stung from dryness and his head pounded. His tongue felt like it was at least four sizes to big for his mouth.

"OI." Ollie slammed the file into the back of his head. Jack jerked up.

"Fuck off, Ollie! You and I both know this is bullshit."

"What I know," Heath said slowly, "is that I've waited a very long time to get you in the box, Winter. Now I'm going to get answers out of you." He shoved back and stood up. Jack noted his shoes made a gushy sound. "But first, I'm going to get a cup of tea..." Ollie leaned over and tightened the cuffs one more notch, "and then I'm going to fuck you straight up the arse and into Pentonville, where you belong."

"Charmed," Jack muttered. "But you're not really my type."

Ollie slammed Jack's forehead back into the table and left.

After a time the door opened again, and a uniformed plod came in. Jack's eyes refused to focus. He glared anyway. "You here to work me over, then?"

The plod took a folded piece of white paper from his sleeve and slid it under Jack's cuffed hands. Silently as he'd come, he retreated.

Jack waited until the door had shut, and the unfolded the note. He knew there was a camera on the other side of the mirror that reflected his haggard, hollow-cheeked face back at him, but what else could the Met do to him? He was already good for four murders in their eyes.

The note was simple:

Outside.

Jack looked around, and when he looked at the door it was standing open a crack. His cuffs were still locked to the ring in the table, but handcuffs were simple. Practically the first lock he'd ever slipped had been cuffs.

It could be a trick, he reasoned. But Ollie already knew that he'd do a runner if he got the chance. Maybe Heath was just trying to lure him off Yard property so he could beat seven kinds of shit out of him.

Or it could be someone else entirely.

Think of the person who hates you most in the world, the ghost's voice came back.

Jack didn't take the time to try and remember them all. He pressed his will into the lock, his talent. Locks and Jack understood one another, had since before he'd realized that he had any sort of magic at all. Locks opened under his fingers, lifted their skirts for him, put food on the table and pills down his mum's gullet back in Manchester.

The cuffs didn't give him any trouble.

Jack shed them onto the floor and repeated the process with the door, stepping into the hallway.

The light was the same dour florescence as the interrogation room. At the far end, a fire exit stood with broad warnings to not push the bar unless you wished to sound the alarm.

Jack saw the door had been propped open with a paperweight in the shape of Stonehenge. Pete smoked like a chimney fire when she was at the Met and he wagered it was a quick way to nip out without the DCI noticing.

Jack took the fire stairs down.

He went down until he couldn't go down any more except through a door marked BASEMENT, and then he stepped out into another featureless hallway. A doorway at the far end was a proper exit.

He walked quickly, mindful of the fact that somewhere, someone was watching him on a camera, and then pushed through the door.

It had started to rain while he'd been in the box, the slow, insistent, miserable winter rain that was endemic to London.

It slanted past the lamp over the door and formed rivulets and puddles across the potholed car park.

A man stood a few yards from Jack, hands in his pockets, collar turned up against the rain. He didn't seem to mind it. He seemed to be smiling.

Jack stepped out of the glare of the lamp, water sluicing around his boots. A shear of wind cut around the corner of New Scotland Yard and rocked him in his stead. A true storm was brewing, the kind that blew in from the sea up the Thames Estuary and put London under water. The kind of storm that, before Joseph Bazalgette's modern system installed for Victoria, used to make the sewers overflow and spread cholera and filth.

"Don't worry about the alarms," the man said. "I've put their minds on other things for the moment. Just long enough that you and I can have a talk."

Rain water ran into his eyes, but Jack swiped it away with the back of his hand. He looked at the face in the shadows.

Gavin Lecroix smiled at him. "Hello, Jack. It's been far too long."

eighteen

FOR a long time, heartbeats, Jack simply stared. Rain worked down the back of his neck, down his shirt, soaking him with cold and wet borne from the sea. "Gavin," he said. That was all he could think of.

Gavin's face had gotten thinner, longer, older. Jack supposed his own had too. "You?" That was progress. He didn't get shocks very often. Not real ones, and they'd been coming thick and fast over the past forty-eight hours.

"You know," Gavin said. "I asked you, all that time ago. I said 'Take me with you, Jack.' Do you remember what you said to me?"

Jack felt himself starting to shiver. The air between him and Gavin snapped with cold, the rain crystallizing and falling to the ground like shattered glass.

He did remember.

"'Fuck off, Gavin,'" Gavin said, Jack's lips moving in time. "'This world ain't for you.'"

"I *had* the knack," Gavin said. "And you knew it, and you put me off anyway. You left me to fend for myself, Jack. You swanned off on your grand adventure and you left me alone like scraps. You want to know what picked me up?"

"Not particularly, mate," Jack said. His throat was curiously tight, like he'd swallowed a smooth round stone. He'd never bothered to catch up with Gavin again. Gavin was, if Jack were honest and not merely nostalgic, the kind of guy who always stared a little too long and acted a little too eager to take the drunken girls from the pit backstage. It didn't always matter if they were conscious. Gavin and Dix had nearly come to blows one night. Just after that show in Birmingham, where Jack had met Fiona and was too busy getting his cock sucked to realize Gavin had pulled a knife on his drummer.

Fucking Gavin. Always just a bit off of center.

"Guess," Gavin snarled. "You know what happened to me, Winter. You know exactly what kind of people would want a mixed-up boy like me."

Jack swiped the rain off his face. He couldn't feel his hands. Gavin's cold was closing him off, shutting down his senses one by one. "Black magic," he said. "That much is obvious."

Gavin smiled. It was all teeth and no lip, a wolf's grin. "Always were the master of the obvious, Jack. Subtle as a brick to the head, and spilling over with that ego that wouldn't let you admit someone else might be a bit more inclined to the talent than you. That's the real reason you dropped me like a hot coal. Couldn't take the chance I'd eclipse the great Jack Winter."

Jack breathed in, out. The cold sliced his lungs like knives. He had to get control of this, like Pete would if a crazy bugger were standing with a knife to his own throat. "The talent you're getting stiff over was barely an itch in those days," he said. "I didn't need a fucking apprentice. And honestly, Gavin, you were always a bit of a fuckwit."

Gavin tilted his head. "Suppose I was. I was young. But you, Jack..." Gavin took a step forward, and then Jack found himself on his back, skull ringing on the icy pavement. Gavin's hand was sure and strong, closed around his neck. "You were always too bloody arrogant to have any survival instincts."

With his free hand, Gavin took out a black marker from his jacket pocket, and ripped Jack's shirt open. "I worshiped you," he whispered, pressing the point into Jack's flesh. "I wanted to *be* you, drink your magic down until I was full. But when you left I learned there are far worse things out there than the crow-mage."

Gavin drew surely, the same symbol he'd tried to slap on Jack earlier, by proxy. "Rather pedestrian, don't you think?" he croaked. "A Sharpie, in the car park? The blood and the spooky cellar had a lot more of a theatrical edge, Gav."

Gavin smiled at him again, and hit him in the mouth. Flashbulbs exploded behind Jack's eyes, and he found that he couldn't move. Gavin didn't even need a word of power to lay a hex on him. Unless he got him flustered, got his mind off whatever insane revenge trip he was traveling, Jack knew he was fucked, good and proper.

"So," he said, relieved he could still talk. "Ghosts, then? Murder the pathetic sods who bind ghosts, take them for yourself? Give you more juice to work your pathetic little revenge? For what, Gavin? You going to fuck over every bloke who didn't want to be friends, one by one?"

"There are people in the Black who are organized, Jack," Gavin said, humming as he added flourishes to his work. Jack's skin, both hot and cold at once, felt as if it were going to strip off his skeleton and dance on its own. "'Course, you wouldn't know about that. You're like a fucking Bon Jovi song, the great lone mage. But those organized people and I will be making alliances when they see how I've bound four spirits to those other bastard's one, and then…yes, I suppose I will be able to pull out the teeth and burn the bones of everyone who's ever wronged me. If I like."

Gavin sat back on his heels, and looked at the sky. "Now, they'll come. For you. I have to say, Jack, this was a nice bit of side work. I get to take my ghosts and fuck you over all at once."

"You could have just let me go to prison," Jack protested. "This sorcery shite really isn't necessary."

"Yeah," Gavin said tightly. "You would think that." He stood up, stretched, rolled his neck. The rain fell all around, but it avoided him, as if he was made of flame.

"Then why?" Jack demanded. His voice was sliding up the scale. He wasn't rattling Gavin. He wasn't even mildly perturbing Gavin. The man was focused as a monk.

"You don't remember," Gavin murmured, and for the first time his face went slack, something beside that ice-carved sociopath's grin crawling across his visage. "I asked you, in the pub—well, Matthew Killian did—and you don't remember. You honestly don't think you did anything wrong." Gavin's mouth twisted. "The fit-up wasn't just for me. It was for every sad groupie and normal bloke you've ever fucked over. You've got a nice life, Winter, and you don't deserve it."

Of course, Jack thought. Killian, with the strand of power under his skin Jack couldn't identify. A glamour, cooked up to let Gavin close with his odd questions. The cup of coffee, that Gavin had undoubtedly nicked Jack's fingerprints and DNA from while he was busy revising history to make himself look ice cold and devil-may-care.

Maybe the ponce was right. Jack thought in that moment that ego might actually get him good and killed.

No. Jack clenched his jaw, forced himself not to thrash and panic, try to throw his magic against Gavin's. It wouldn't do any good. The bastard was more powerful, and he was in his element.

"I guess I was wrong," he said, the words rushing forth. "I was wrong to not at least teach you a few things, just like I was wrong to not try and really help Fiona. I've done so much wrong, Gavin, sometimes it gets hard to remember it all. Just pile another stone on. I'm sorry, mate. You think I have a good life, but it's shit even without a murder rap. If you can't see that, then really. I'm truly sorry."

Gavin held up a finger, like he was shushing a roomful of students. "Here he comes."

Rasputin didn't materialize—he was simply there, like a bad dream. Raindrops passed through him, sizzling as they hit the pavement.

You, he hissed. *What do you think you'll do to me?*

"Bind you," Gavin said surely. "Look, I brought you a snack and everything. Recharge. You've been drifting for days now."

"See?" Jack said. "Told you he was a shifty git."

I will not be bound, Rasputin said. *You promised to let me go.*

"I lied," Gavin said, lifting one shoulder. "And there's not fuck all you can do about it. You're the last—I already have your mates under my thumb. So either stand for the binding or I'm going to use this silly git here to blow you sky high." The smile was back. "I can siphon out his power just like you can, Grigorii. Good trick. Crowley showed me."

"Hate to be the one to sound the broken record," Jack said to the mad monk. "But I told you. You going to stand for that?"

"Shut it!" Gavin snapped. He tucked his chin to his chest and mumbled a word of power, and three other ghosts shimmered into existence amid the snow that was drifting gently over the car park, transformed by Gavin's power. Jack recognized Crowley, but the other two were simply the memories of men, one in a tunic that looked as if it had escaped a Faire, and the other in what appeared to be pyjamas and a nightcap, sporting a Gandalf beard.

You'd turn against me, Rasputin murmured. *That I knew. But you did not seem a coward, who uses dead men for his dirty work.*

"Bad luck for you, then," Gavin said. "Because I'm exactly that sort of coward." He said another word of power, and Jack waited for the ghosts to fall on Rasputin, and then him.

Nobody moved. Just the snow, falling and drifting to crystallize on Jack's eyelashes, turning his world into a fractal view of Gavin and his ghosts.

Rasputin began to laugh. *It seems you have their spirits,* he said, *but not their loyalty.*

Crowley looked down at Jack with a small smile. *I did rather like you, my dear,* he whispered. *This git, not nearly as amusing.*

"Fine!" Gavin snarled. "You think I won't get my hands dirty, Rasputin? You're sorely fucking mistaken."

Gavin flew at the ghost, and Jack would spend hours, in the pub with glass after glass of whiskey, puzzling over just what happened next. He'd seen a lot of things—Santeria priests speaking with the fiery tongues of saints, *loa* spirits walking amongst the dancers in a voodoo ceremony, the Baron Samedi tipping his hat to the recently departed, Stygian brothers birthing their great tentacle beasts from the body cavities of living, willing victims, but he'd never seen anything quite like what happened when Gavin touched Rasputin's ghost.

They *meshed,* was the best way Jack could describe it, Gavin opening his mouth and sinking his teeth into Rasputin's spectral flesh. Rasputin screamed, or perhaps Gavin screamed, or perhaps Jack did, as his sight split apart and he saw Rasputin as he'd seen Crowley—a skull with flaming black eyes, matted, decomposing hair, hands with steel hooks for claws, clinging desperately to the Black.

Gavin—Gavin was nothing. He was a howling void of magic, a black, sucking thing that was nothing but rage and hunger.

Jack saw then that whatever had been Gavin had died a long time ago. What was riding his soul now was nothing that had ever been human.

Rasputin fought him, claws and teeth tearing off chunks, but it wasn't enough. The Gavin-thing sucked him in, turned him into a butterfly on a board, pinned and thrashing. Gavin's ice cold, unearthly magic ate up everything around it. The Black, Jack's sight, and soon his sanity, but he couldn't move and couldn't close his eyes.

"You see, Jack?" the Gavin-thing screamed. "You see what you made? Are you proud, Jack? Are you—"

Jack never discovered what he was supposed to be. There were three thunderclaps, short and tight together, and lighting, and then the snow was no longer white but painted with a long streak of red.

Gavin's corporeal body pitched forward. The howling thing lifted and separated from him, and still battling with Rasputin, disappeared into the Black.

Jack choked as all of his muscles abruptly came back under his control. Gavin's power was gone, and Gavin's ghosts with it. They were alone in the car park except for Ollie Heath, who came forward and nudged Gavin with his foot. His 9mm pistol was beginning to look almost natural in his pudgy hand.

He looked down at Jack, mouth curled. "You are fuckin' lucky," Ollie told him, "that I am a great bloody shot."

nineteen

"HOW much did you hear?" Jack asked, when Ollie helped him to his feet, and called for uniforms and a crime scene team to care for Gavin's body.

"Enough," Ollie said. "I was standing there for a bit, trying to puzzle out why you were in the car park and I couldn't remember the last bloody ten minutes of my life."

"You stood there long enough for Gavin to almost rip me fucking face off?" Jack said. "You couldn't have, I don't know, filled him full of lead a few minutes earlier?"

Ollie shrugged. "I needed good evidence. And you looked as if you were handling things." His mouth twitched, but he stuck out his hand. "I was wrong about you, Winter. But you still owe me a new pair of fucking shoes."

After a few hours, when Jack had given a proper statement about Gavin Lecroix, Ollie let him go. It was still coming down snow when he left the station. Ollie had offered to call Pete, but Jack insisted he was fine to walk to the tube.

He wasn't fine. Gavin had stalked him, murdered four people, tried to bind four ghosts to himself, fit Jack for murder. All because he thought Jack a fucking bastard undeserving of what, in Gavin's magic-crazed eyes, was a shining life.

Because he *was* a fucking bastard. Jack usually took pride in the fact. He watched a cab swish by on the snowy road, yellow roof sign disappearing into the night like a firefly, and he didn't feel any pride at all. Fiona shouldn't have died. Gavin shouldn't have been turned into some kind of half-human husk of nightmare. And, Jack considered, if he could pull back from the shouldn'ts and the positively Catholic guilt he felt over Fiona, he did have a life. He had a flat, he had his dubious health, fags and whiskey, music and takeaway. He had Pete. He had, double edged blade though it could be, a talent the normal sort of bloke could only imagine.

Gavin had been right. On balance, Jack didn't deserve a fucking bit of it.

He rode the tube, barely seeing where he was putting his feet, got off and climbed up the stairs to the Mile End Road.

Ginger Annie was on her corner. She smiled at him, and reached out her hand. Jack stopped.

"Oh, my love," she said. "You look awful. Just awful."

"I'm a tosser, Annie," Jack said. "People do terrible, terrible things in my name. I bring out the worst in them, like I'm some kind of bloody magnet for the darker half."

Annie considered him for a moment. "Who died, Jack?"

"A friend," Jack said. "An old friend," he amended. "And a girl I used to know. And so many people before that, Annie. Too many to count."

She held up one hand to the snow. It fell through her kid-gloved palm. "You know what a lot of people said when McReady stove my head in? Said I had it coming. 'Cos of what I did, what I was." She stopped staring up at the falling flakes and looked at him instead. "Some of us walk the dark road, Jack. It doesn't mean we've got a dark heart inside of us." She touched him, and Jack let her. He couldn't get colder. He and Annie, at that moment, were nearly the same. "Whatever you did," Annie whispered. "It wasn't because you're rotten, Jack. The world is rotten. And some can pretend it isn't, and some…" She dropped her hand. "Some see it how it is."

Jack thought of Fiona, lying very still on her table in the mortuary. The pain in Gavin's voice when he said Jack had forgotten.

"And ain't it a fucking paradise," he said to Annie.

"You'll keep walking," Annie said. "Your kind always do."

Jack started walking again, for his flat. Pete was waiting, probably going out of her mind. "Thanks, Annie," he said over his shoulder.

She had already forgotten about him. Annie could never walk on, dark road or no.

Jack left her where she was. Just as she couldn't move, he couldn't stay. Otherwise, memory would eat him alive.

twenty

PETE didn't say much, other than to ask him if he was all right. Jack discovered he'd gotten Gavin's blood on him. He pulled off his stolen shirt and told Pete, "Burn this fucking thing."

She made him tea with a slug of whiskey while Jack ran a bath from the arthritic faucet. He let himself soak for a long time, while Pete sat on the lid of the toilet and they talked, about everything. He told her about Fiona before, when he'd left her with Chester. Gemma, and how she'd been the closest thing he'd had to a friend for so long, and he'd repaid her by smashing her life to bits. About Gavin. How it had almost all come to a close in the car park of the Met.

Pete got down onto the bath rug and put her hands on his shoulders. "Jack," she said. "That bastard made his call. You think he wouldn't have found another excuse?"

"He didn't need one," Jack muttered.

"Bullshit," Pete said crisply. "He went after you, Jack, because you'll take the weight on. You'll admit to the bad as easily as the good. You'll be responsible for all the black things that other people try to hide. And that's not a flaw, Jack. That's a fucking bit of your soul." She pressed her lips to his forehead. "You're not a wicked man, Jack Winter. You do wicked things for a reason. Maybe a shit reason from time to time, but you know your road. It's different than what Gavin tried to make you think."

Standing, she got him a towel and then went into the hallway. "I'm going to bed," she said. "This whole business has me fucking knackered." Pausing, she looked over her shoulder. "You can come in tonight, if you like. I think I need to know that you're still here."

Jack nodded. He couldn't even muster up a dirty reply. "Be just a bit," he said. Pete disappeared into her bedroom and Jack dried himself off, but instead of going to bed, curling himself around Pete's small body and using her to get warm, he went to the bookcases in the sitting room.

The cardboard box was where he'd left it, amid the clutter on the top shelf, detritus from decades of forgetting. He left hand prints in the dust on the lid, and had to unplug the telly to find an outlet for the reel-to-reel player, but at last he sat on the sofa and lit a fag, and put on the old earphones with the stuffing leaking out.

The master reels of *Nightmares and Strange Days* were scratched and worn in spots—Jack supposed he should digitize the lot and throw the musty things away, or sell them to some twenty-year-old who'd wet himself at the very idea of touching the scratched plastic reels and failing tape.

He flipped the player's switch and sat back. His own voice came out of the earphones, scratched and muffled with age. The first verse of "Cross Styx," the song Gavin had hated the most out of their entire set list.

"Got a black river down in the depths of my soul
Filled with a tide that comes and it goes..."

Jack moved his fingers on his towel-clad leg as Dix kicked in with the drumline. Rich's guitar was hard and chopped, dry as a desert, the whole thing pared down and sharp, the Bauhaus with a boot in their face, Jack finding a Mark Knopfler growl he hadn't known he possessed until he stepped up to the recording mike.

He let his cigarette burn down in his fingers as the years fell away. Gavin had hated the song. Hated him. Blamed him.

Jack dragged and exhaled, and for a moment he had his own ghost. It was gone in the space of half a heartbeat. He didn't need any more ghosts. He saw enough without taking on Gavin and Fiona as well.

Settling back as the track changed, to the pure anarchy and chord-crunching riot of "Mistress Knives", Jack knew that eventually he'd go in to Pete, and he'd let the ghost of Gavin slip away. He'd convince himself Gavin had been wrong, and that Jack enjoyed being a bastard after all.

But for the moment, he stayed where he was, smoked and remembered, and listened to the music, just himself and his ghosts, in the dark.